Allyson James

Rees Tales of the Shareem

ELLORA'S CAVE
ROMANTICA PUBLISHING

An Ellora's Cave Romantica Publication

www.ellorascave.com

Rees

ISBN 1419952252, 9781419952555
ALL RIGHTS RESERVED.
Rees Copyright © 2005 Allyson James
Edited by Heather Osborn.
Cover art by Syneca.

This book printed in the U.S.A. by Jasmine-Jade Enterprises, LLC.

Electronic book Publication March 2005
Trade paperback Publication September 2005

Also by Allyson James

ॐ

Christmas Cowboy

Double Trouble

Ellora's Cavemen: Dreams of the Oasis I (*anthology*)

Ellora's Cavemen: Seasons of Seduction I (*anthology*)

Tales of the Shareem 2: Maia and Rylan

Tales of the Shareem 3: Rio

Tales of the Shareem 4: Aiden and Ky

About the Author

ഇ

Allyson James is yet one more name for a woman who has racked up four pseudonyms in the first two years of her career. She often cannot remember what her real name is and has to be tapped on the shoulder when spoken to.

Allyson began writing at age eight (a five-page story that actually contained goal, motivation, and conflict). She learned the trick of standing her math book up on her desk so she could write stories behind it. She wrote love stories before she knew what romances were, dreaming of the day when her books would appear at libraries and bookstores. At age thirty, she decided to stop dreaming and do it for real. She published the first short story she ever submitted in a national print magazine, which gave her the false illusion that getting published was easy.

After a long struggle and inevitable rejections, she at last sold a romance novel, then, to her surprise, sold several mystery novels, more romances, and then Romantica™ to Ellora's Cave. She has been nominated for two Romantic Times Reviewer's Choice awards and has had starred reviews in *Booklist* and Top Pick reviews in *Romantic Times*.

Allyson met her soulmate in fencing class (the kind with swords, not posts-and-rails). She looked down the length of his long, throbbing rapier and fell madly in love.

Allyson welcomes comments from readers. You can find her website and email address on her author bio page at www.ellorascave.com.

Tell Us What You Think

We appreciate hearing reader opinions about our books. You can email us at Comments@EllorasCave.com.

REES
Tales of the Shareem

ഇ

Chapter One

ഔ

A Shareem male.

Easy to tell he was Shareem, first because he was tall, more than six and a half feet. Second, because of the slim black chain on his left biceps. Third, because he was naked, except for a loincloth around his waist.

From the other side of the airy white hall, Talan watched the Shareem pause in front of the door to a holo-block.

The Shareem had long hair, dark blond and pulled into a tail that hung between his shoulder blades. His back muscles were sculpted to perfection, tapering to a small waist and muscular thighs.

The loincloth left his backside bare. Talan had never seen a man's backside before. It was enough to dry her mouth and start her juices flowing.

Reading about Shareem was one thing. Researching in a dusty library was one thing. Seeing a Shareem in the flesh was something completely different.

She knew now why women had once gone crazy trying to get them.

Shareem. Genetically enhanced males, grown and bred for the pleasure of females. A craze twenty years ago, very illegal these days.

Despite the cooling system inside Talan's robes, sweat trickled down her back.

He paid for the holo-block with a credit strip, and the big door slid open. Beyond, Talan glimpsed an ocean, palm trees and a beach. Good choice.

The Shareem entered the room. The door started to close.

Talan had never broken a rule in her life. Talan d'Urvey would never, ever sneak into a holo-block rented for only one person. That would be wrong.

But she'd followed him this far, and she could not linger for hours waiting for him to come out.

The door had nearly closed. Talan flung herself across the hall and into the holo-room just before the door boomed shut behind her.

Rees stared out across the blue-green waves of the tropical ocean, sank his toes into the warm sand, and thought about the woman following him.

Rees liked oceans. The desert world of Bor Narga had no oceans, except for a dried-up one in the middle of the planet.

He liked the soothing cool of the water and the tropical air touching his ass, kissing his skin like a woman's lips. It was a perfect place to ponder the problem Rio had brought to him and to think about the woman.

She'd been following him all morning, ever since he'd left the bazaar. At first he'd thought she was a patroller, one of that fine body of women who enjoyed harassing the now-free Shareem.

A closer glance told him no. Her robes placed her as upper-class. The patterns and colors on them indicated she was unmarried, educated, and celibate.

A celibate young woman following a Shareem.

He wanted to laugh. *Naughty girl.*

She'd followed him into the holo-block then dived for cover behind the broad-leafed plants and stayed there.

Maybe he should give her a show. He could stretch out on the sand, place his hand on his thigh and brace his cock so it would point straight to the sky. He'd spread his legs a little, show her that his balls were tight and lifting for her.

The DNAmo programmers had designed Shareem to respond to even subtle stimulation. Just being watched by an interested woman could make his cock rise.

Besides, she was cute.

He imagined her coming out from her hiding place, kneeling and taking him in her mouth.

Mmm, he wanted that.

A celibate wouldn't know what to do. He'd have to show her. His cock tingled in anticipation.

She must not know what he was, or she'd have run away as fast as her high-heeled boots would let her.

She should have picked a level one Shareem to follow. Level ones were pretty harmless. Even level twos could be fun, if a lady enjoyed, say, a little spanking.

Level threes could get even more creative.

Rees was a level all by himself.

Even ladies used to Shareem said Rees was dangerous. They said it with an excited tremor in their voices.

Rees was one of the reasons Shareem were taboo now. He'd been an experiment, a risk, *a step too far*, some said.

One day he'd heard the scientists say that they needed to terminate the *experiment*. He'd been pretty sure how they were going to do that.

He'd gotten away, and the next week the company went bankrupt. DNAmo, who'd thrived for a hundred years breeding the perfect servants and then the perfect males, disappeared.

People had looked for Rees at first, then had forgotten about him. They believed the DNAmo scientists had fled with him. No one even knew what he looked like.

Rio knew. Rees knew. A few women thought they knew, but couldn't be sure.

And here he was.

He could taste the lady's pheromones on the air. She was wet and wanting him.

Well, she'd get what she came for. She should learn not to play with fire.

He turned around and made for her hiding place in the greenery. He'd give her a chance to leave. That was only fair.

He stopped right in front of her. Between the broad, flat leaves behind which she crouched, her fire-colored hair and transparent veil nestled like a flower.

"Come on out," he said.

The figure didn't move.

"You're not really hiding," Rees said, trying not to laugh. "I see you."

She quivered a second, then slowly stood up.

Rees took a stunned step back. Did he say *cute*? She was gorgeous.

Red hair framed the round face of a woman in her early twenties. Thick, black lashes enhanced the bluest eyes he'd ever seen. He imagined her fluttering those lashes over his lips, over his balls…

Her robes mostly hid her, but he could see the swell of breasts and the round of her hips and backside. He liked imagining what she looked like under all that fabric. He'd like to take off those robes, layer by slow layer.

"Well?" he said.

"Well, what?" She was trying to be snooty, but she was too nervous.

"Why are you following me?"

She got more nervous. "I thought this room was empty."

Liar. He laughed. "No, you didn't."

Another thing enhanced on a Shareem was his voice. He could soothe a woman just by saying hello, make her shiver by saying her name.

The woman looked anything but soothed. "I thought— I did not mean to— It's all right, I'll leave."

She swung around, robes whirling in the tropical breeze. He caught her arm. She turned, startled, then she glared at him.

A Shareem never touched an upper-class woman without her permission. It wasn't done.

His friend Rio, a level three and not ashamed of it, did it all the time.

"I'm just a badass," Rio would say. Rio would have already lifted this lady's skirts and showed her what a level three could do.

Rees was a little kinder.

"I can think of only one reason a celibate woman would follow a Shareem," Rees said.

She blinked. "Oh? Why?"

He lowered his voice, made it still more seductive. "Because she wants her first fuck. Why else?"

She looked at him in amazement, and her face turned bright red. "Of course not."

"You didn't follow me to play hide and seek. You're celibate. You want me to make you un-celibate."

"No, no," she said. "I will go to a clinic for that."

Upper-class women had clinics for sexual health and for donating DNA to make children. None of them had anything to do with sex.

Not swollen cock in hot, slippery pussy kind of sex anyway.

"Then what?"

She blushed. "I just wanted to see a Shareem."

He spread his arms. "Here I am."

She made no pretense of not looking. Those blue eyes moved as she examined him from his blond hair all the way down his muscled chest and flat stomach, his thighs and calves and bare feet.

Her gaze rose again, lingered on the loincloth, which was bulging, and landed on the black chain on his biceps.

"Do you mind being a slave?" she asked.

"Shareem aren't slaves," he said. "We do what we want." *Mostly.*

"But you were made in a factory."

"Grown in a vat, yeah. But here we are."

She looked him up and down one more time, fascinated. "You're not what I expected."

"What did you expect?"

"You're human," she said, in wonder. "I didn't think you'd be so human."

That stunned him. Most women looked no farther than his huge cock and didn't much care about anything else.

He wasn't considered human. Humanoid, maybe.

Something in his heart warmed a tiny bit. He should be kind to her. Let her get away.

No. Hunt her through the brush and out into the waves –

He stopped the thought. "You shouldn't have followed me. A level one, maybe. But not me."

Her brows rose. "Why not?"

"Because I'm Rees."

Her look told him she'd never heard of him. "What is a Rees?"

She made him laugh, lucky for her. The rest of his body screamed at him to throw her down and fuck her and get it over with.

"That's my name."

Her cheeks got red again. "Oh."

He laughed out loud. "Don't worry about it, babe. Come and swim with me," he suggested, pitching his voice to seduce. "The water's nice."

"No, I can't. Thank you for asking, but I'm not ready."

She breathed fast, pushing her delectable breasts up and down.

"Not ready for what?"

"For swimming. Or anything else. My research isn't complete."

"Research?"

"On Shareem."

He stared at her. "You're doing research on Shareem? What is there to research?"

"Oh, many, many things."

He wanted to laugh again.

He wouldn't mind helping with a little research. He'd pull off his loincloth, lay her on the sand, lace his fingers through her warm, red hair. Then spread her legs, thrust his tongue inside her fine pussy. Yes, any research was fine with him.

She stammered, "I wondered if you would—ah—"

He leaned closer. She had a sweet scent overlaid with a tang of excited woman.

What do you want me to do, love? he thought. *Fuck you? Lick you? Fill your mouth?*

Bind her hands, part her legs. Take…

Again, he stopped his thoughts. She was celibate and clueless. She had no idea what he could do, what Shareem could do, what *Rees* could do.

The woman drew a breath. "I wonder if you'd give me a sample of your DNA."

Rees stared at her. "Okay, I've had bizarre requests before, but... What do you want to do? Grow your own Shareem? That's illegal, darling."

"No, no. I only want to look at it. To see what's different about you."

"What's different is I don't have parents. Or, maybe I have multiple parents. Or scientists with nothing better to do."

She frowned, like she didn't know what he was talking about.

"What's your name?" he asked.

She wet her lips. "Talan."

"Pretty name for a lady researcher. Okay, Talan, you can have my DNA. Mind if I think of some fun ways of giving it to you?"

"That's all right, I'll just take cells from your finger." She reached into her robe, pulling out something that looked like a sharp knife with a tube attached to it.

Rees took an instinctive step back. Clinics and tubes and knives always bothered him.

"Ready?" she asked.

He made himself hold up his finger. The holo-block sunlight glittered on his tanned skin and the black chain.

As though she saw nothing but his finger, Talan scraped a little of the skin from his fingertip. She closed the tube over the knife and put it back into her pocket. She looked satisfied.

"Is that it?" he asked.

"Yes, thank you. Thank you very much."

"You're welcome."

He should not touch her, he knew that, and not just because it was taboo. She stirred him up, and stirring up Rees was dangerous.

But he *wanted* to touch her. He reached out and brushed a strand of hair from her forehead.

She stared at him, mesmerized. His touch, his voice, his gaze, were all made to melt a woman.

"You're putting a spell on me," she whispered. "I read about that."

He grinned. "I know. I can't help it."

"I have to go."

"So you keep saying."

He withdrew his touch. She drew a sharp breath, as though released from a trap. She whirled around again, making for the door.

"Sure you don't want to stay?" he asked.

She shook her head. "I am already very late. If I have to explain..."

If her friends were the upper-class elite—women who'd decided that good old-fashioned screwing was bad, women who'd made laws restricting Shareem—she would be in for it, all right.

"Tell them you were researching," he called.

"Good idea. Goodbye, Mr. Rees. And thank you."

She turned again, running straight at the wall. Triggered, the door materialized in front of her and opened. She ran through, the draft swirling her robes above a pair of legs that made his blood sing. Then the door whooshed shut.

He stood there for a minute while the tropical air caressed him and the palm trees whispered and the ocean slithered up the beach.

Then he ripped off his loincloth and ran across the beach and into the waves.

His blood pounded and every cell in his body burned. He was like a lava flow in the water. He was surprised the holo-sea didn't start boiling.

It was all he could do not to run after her, haul her back in, lock the door. He'd lay her down, thrust his cock inside her, keep pounding until he came. And she came. And he came again.

But he didn't.

She'd said *thank you*.

Fuck, fuck, fuck!

His cock, enhanced like the rest of him, stood out straight, even in the cool water.

Thank gods he'd decided to do an ocean. If he'd picked the garden with the fountain, he'd be dead, because no way a little trickling fountain would cool him down.

He plunged underwater, letting the waves slither over his naked body. It helped—some. He pictured the woman, Talan, coming back in, throwing off her robes, swimming out to him, twining her arms around his neck.

He'd lower his head and kiss her lips.

That wasn't helping.

When he surfaced, blood still pounding, the pheromone levels in the room had decreased slightly—probably saving him from an early death. His heartbeat finally settled down.

It took his cock longer to deflate, but disappointment helped.

He floated on his back, thinking.

He'd remember her face. He'd see her again.

Once he'd finished helping Rio, he'd seek her out. An upper-class woman called Talan wouldn't be too hard to find.

And when he did, he'd remind her of the lost opportunity they'd had here on the tropical beach.

The fucking would be good, he thought, his cock throbbing again. *It would be very good.* He knew it in his bones.

Chapter Two
Two weeks later

๛

"Following the Way of the Star means separating mind and body," the lecturer continued in her dulcet tones. "The mind can only function at its highest level if we leave the ways of the body behind. The flesh is ugly, it is heavy, it keeps us pinned to lesser things."

Talan, kneeling amidst the other students of the Way, reflected that the Shareem's flesh certainly hadn't been ugly.

She remembered his sculpted back, his tight backside, the dark blue of his eyes.

No, definitely not ugly.

But then, Shareem had been programmed to be perfect.

Soft air wafted through the artificially cool room scented with sandalwood. The lecturer, an older woman with a voice like mellow wood, droned on.

Talan had always loved her time of learning and meditation in the school of her Way, but after she'd met the Shareem, she'd had a hard time concentrating.

These ladies had no idea, she thought, glancing at their closed eyes, bowed heads, and furrowed brows. They had not read Lady Ursula's diary. They had never seen a Shareem male.

Magnificently tall, broad of shoulder, strong, sexual.

He embodied everything forbidden in the Way of the Star. Everything shunned by modern philosophy.

Bor Narga was a highly advanced civilization. In a time when people could manipulate genetics and produce children outside a woman's body, coupling was unnecessary. Sex had been deemed animalistic. Thinking humans did not need it.

Sex, in fact, took away from the better things in life. One needed a clear head to meditate and study and write. Sexual appetites pulled a woman down.

A woman could still marry and have children, of course. She would seek a man who wanted a marriage of minds, and then they'd donate their DNA to the Ministry of Families to create a pleasing child.

A woman did not need carnality.

Or Shareem.

Talan had been perfectly happy to follow her path. She liked the Way and the friends she'd made in it.

Until she'd found the diary.

Lady Ursula d'Mato of the Way of the Star had spent one sinful week twenty years ago with a Shareem called Brandt. He'd taught her many, many things, and she'd written all about them in her diary. The descriptions had been earthy and most detailed.

Lady Ursula had started her week with mild curiosity and had finished it never wanting it to stop.

They diary had broken off after she'd left for her last encounter with Brandt. There were no further entries and no more records of Lady Ursula after that.

Talan had asked her foster mother, Lady Petronella, if she knew what had become of the woman, but Lady Pet didn't know. She hadn't known Lady Ursula very well and had assumed the woman had moved off-planet.

The diary had given Talan strange dreams. She'd dream of a Shareem doing the things Lady Ursula described.

He'd strip the coverings off the bed, Talan's nightclothes from her body. He'd lick the underside of her arm, then the inside of her thighs. He'd touch her with fingers sensuous and slow.

Talan would wake up with her own fingers pressing against her opening and her cream everywhere.

She'd wanted to see a real Shareem, just to look at one.

And so when she'd spotted the Shareem—Rees—she'd felt compelled to follow him.

Talan had thought a Shareem would be different. More alien. More bizarre than the normal human male, certainly.

But he'd been so *real*. He smelled real and looked real and felt real.

Her reaction when he looked at her had completely unnerved her.

He had suggested so casually that she'd followed him because she wanted her first fuck. Her nipples had tightened, and her cream had started to flow.

A Shareem could trick a woman with his touch and his voice, but this one hadn't needed to try very hard.

When he'd asked her to come for a swim, she'd had to stop her arms from flinging off her clothes and her feet from running out into the ocean.

She'd imagined the cool water caressing her naked skin, imagined him smiling a Shareem smile at her, imagined him reaching for her. The feeling called lust had woken up and waved for her attention.

Her reaction made her realize she'd easily given up carnality because she'd never felt it before. Easy to give up sweets if you've never tasted any.

Talan had been a voyeur to Lady Ursula's one forbidden week. She'd wanted to see more.

And now, she wanted to experience what Lady Ursula had.

She looked out of the corners of her eyes to the ladies around her. They had no idea what she was thinking, they did not know that her cream was flowing just remembering the Shareem and his smile.

The Shareem's touch had softened her mind, opened it.

There in that lecture room, while her beloved teacher began the chant about giving up bodily pleasure, Talan made her decision.

"Lady Pet," Talan said that night at home.

Lady Petronella d'Naris set her silver fork on the china plate, brought all the way from Earth. Lady Petronella always insisted on the best.

"Yes, dear?"

"I met a Shareem."

Lady Pet's crystal wineglass froze halfway to her mouth. "You *did*?"

"Yes. Two weeks ago."

Lady Pet raised her brows, set down the wineglass. "Talan, you naughty girl, you never told me. Did you like him?" She waved her hand. "What am I saying, of course you did. No one is dissatisfied with a Shareem."

Talan's face grew hot. "I didn't mean I had sex with him," she said quickly. "I met him. I talked to him."

"Talked? Talan, you don't *talk* to a Shareem. That's not what they're for."

"I did."

Lady Pet sighed. "You are the oddest girl I ever raised."

"I'm the only girl you ever raised," Talan pointed out.

"I know that. And I've failed utterly. Else you'd not have fallen into this odd philosophy twaddle, and think you are supposed to *talk* to a Shareem." She shuddered. "Ladies didn't think that way in my day. We *liked* men. What is the world coming to?"

She went silent a moment, then her eyes widened. "Oh, dear, you did not try to preach your no-appetite philosophy to a Shareem, did you? I hope he didn't know you were *my* foster daughter."

"No." Talan turned her wineglass uneasily. She had confided her encounter to no one, not even Lady Pet, who had embarrassingly rabid appetites and didn't mind talking about sex.

"I did not really know *what* to say to him. I just babbled."

"Well, never mind what you said. What did he say?"

Talan frowned. "I don't really remember. What he said seems so unimportant, now, but at the time, I was riveted. Does that make sense?"

"Of course. They can charm you just by saying hello. That's how they were programmed." She licked her lips. "How delicious."

"I am researching them," Talan said.

"Researching? Talan, you *are* strange."

Talan had loaded the Shareem's DNA into her computer. The monitor had obligingly shown her pretty helixes, color-enhanced by the program.

Rees' DNA had not looked different from a human's. She'd compared it to her own and to that of one of Lady Pet's male servants. They had all looked remarkably the same.

"They are as human as we are," she said slowly.

"Well, I know that." Lady Pet picked up her wineglass again. "They have manipulated DNA, not completely different. People who say they aren't human tell you that because they are afraid of Shareem. And sex."

"I want to meet one."

"You just said you did."

"I didn't mean like that." Talan flushed. She could not continue.

Lady Pet smiled suddenly. "I am proud of you, Talan."

Talan blinked. "Why?"

"For not being narrow-minded. I suppose you would like this Shareem you've already met?"

"His name is Rees," she said, her throat dry.

Lady Pet picked up her fork. "Would you like me to find him for you?"

"Yes," Talan said hoarsely.

"Excellent. Anything to keep you from bleating about how women don't need to have sex." She started eating again.

Talan did not rise to the bait. She drank her wine, feeling flushed and at the same time excited.

If anyone could find one Shareem in a teeming city of millions, it was Lady Pet. She'd bring Rees home for Talan and gloat about it.

Talan believed in her Way, and she wanted to follow it. But she wanted to know, just briefly, like Lady Ursula, what it was she'd give up.

A small dose of carnality, and then nothing, forever.

She shivered. She didn't know why. But in Rees' eyes, there had been something.

Dangerous.

Nonsense, she thought. He would be here, in her home. With Lady Pet and servants nearby. How dangerous could he be?

But something still made her uneasy.

The way he smiled. The way he said her name. The way he invited her to swim.

She had a feeling she would either regret this, or treasure the memory for the rest of her life.

Probably both.

* * * * *

"So what have you got for me?" Rio asked.

Rio, a level three Shareem, stood six foot seven and had black hair and Shareem-blue eyes. He liked to wear black leather.

"I'm working on it," Rees said.

They were in the bazaar. Acrid scents of spices and incense floated to them. One stall held a jumble of computer and robot parts sold by a man who insisted they'd work with just a little fix-up.

The stalls opened from each vendor's caravan. They were collapsible, so that when an inevitable sandstorm blew through, the vendors could quickly slide everything back into the caravan, don their breath masks and huddle inside to wait it out.

Everyone carried a breath mask, fully charged. To get caught in a sandstorm without one meant certain death.

"I want off this rock," Rio said under his breath.

Rees gave him a look, but no one had heard.

Rio's problem was simple. Shareem were not allowed off Bor Narga, and Rio wanted to go.

Most Shareem came to Rees with their problems. He was not their leader by any means, but he knew people. He knew people who knew people. And he could get people to do things for him.

"I know," Rees said. "But it's not simple."

"I know it's not simple," Rio growled. "I never said it was simple."

"So shut up and let me work on it."

Rio gave him a look, but shut his mouth, thank the gods. The last thing Rees needed was for them both to be arrested for even talking about leaving the planet.

Women gave them sidelong looks as they passed. Rio grinned back at them.

Rio's motto was, *have whip, will use it. Anytime, anywhere. Just ask me.*

These ladies looked like they wanted to ask him.

"Come with me," Rio suggested to Rees. He was still talking about blasting out of Bor Narga.

Rees considered digitals he'd seen of cool green worlds, long sandy beaches and mountains reaching to the sky.

Bor Narga was dry and empty. It had rugged mountains and sand-filled seas. Not much else.

"No," he said. "I like it here."

Rio gave him a look. "You're crazy, you know that?"

He wouldn't understand.

I met a girl.

And what a girl. Rees kept dreaming about her. Long red hair on the pillow, blue eyes heavy with desire. Lips soft on his flesh. Her pretty voice saying his name. Saying thank you.

His dreams were all mixed up. Level one, level two, and level three pleasure fantasies swirled through him one after another.

He wanted to rip off her clothes and fuck her until she screamed. He wanted to slowly slide oil all over her body, listen to her soft voice telling him how much she liked it.

He wanted to tie her to the bed and spank her sweet ass until it was red.

He'd wake up hard and hot and have to spend the rest of the night in his old-fashioned water shower with the temperature set to freezing.

He wasn't getting much sleep.

"So when will you be done working on it?" Rio asked, impatient.

Rees snapped back to the present. "I'm talking to a pilot this afternoon. I'll tell you tonight."

"Meet up at Judith's place?"

Judith ran a bar down in Pas City, the heart of the old town. "Yeah. Works for me."

"Hope you have good news for me, boy-o," Rio growled. "Or I'll have to find a beautiful woman to take it out on."

"And you'll hate every minute of *that*."

Rio laughed. All women within earshot of that Shareem-enhanced laughter turned and sent longing looks at him.

"Watch it," Rees said. "You'll be accused of starting a riot."

Rio's laughter died. "That's why I want out of here," he said in a low voice. "I want to find a place where seventeen women can follow me home without me being accused of disturbing the peace. At least, not until *after* I get home. Then I'll disturb it plenty."

"Your ego is planet-sized," Rees remarked.

"Just like my cock," Rio said smugly.

"I've seen your cock. Don't brag."

"Hey, boy-o. Every time you've seen my cock, it was going in a woman screaming for it."

"Or screaming for you to stop."

Rio laughed again. He never stayed down for long. "They never want me to stop. See you tonight then." He peered at Rees' face. "And get some sleep. You look awful."

Rio walked away, whistling. Shareem could not stay depressed, so went the theory. They could not be deeply hurt, or grieve, or love. In theory.

Rees knew that despite Rio's hot and cold moods, he really did want off Bor Narga. He wanted to go someplace he could be human. Somewhere no one had ever heard of Shareem.

Rio was Rees' best friend, and he'd do what it took to help him.

Rees turned down an alley, heading toward a dock where an unscrupulous woman pilot he knew might be bribed to smuggle out a Shareem. But would she stay bribed and not sell Rio out to the first patrol skimmer that happened by?

That's what he needed to find out.

Rees looked behind him and saw a litter—an upper-class means of transport that floated on an anti-grav hover— surrounded by four burly men, following him.

Unusual. Most upper-class women who wanted the forbidden delights of the Shareem sent for them or smuggled themselves to them. They didn't announce themselves by taking litters into the back streets.

But an upper-class woman had followed him to a rather seedy holo-block just a few weeks ago.

His heart beat faster. *Talan.*

He stopped and politely let the litter catch up to him.

One of the bodyguards, a man who looked like he didn't bother with intelligence, said, "You Rees?"

Generally, Rees would ask who wanted to know. But his whole body knew Talan waited in that litter.

Any minute, she'd pop her head out between the sun-blocking curtains and ask in her sweet voice if he'd come in and fuck her for three days without stopping.

"Yeah, I'm Rees," he said.

The bodyguard gestured to the litter. "Get in."

Rees wasn't stupid. Not usually. But his mind was filled with images of Talan—never-ending, cock-throbbing images. She was in there. He could smell her.

He lifted the sun curtain. The litter was empty.

He took a step back. He opened his mouth to say "Fuck off" but he never got there.

A stun rod bit through his tunic and he crashed against the bodyguard. A black hood went over his head and cold metal locked his wrists together.

The bodyguard shoved Rees into the litter. He only got the "Fff..." out of his mouth before he lost consciousness altogether.

* * * * *

"What did you *do*?"

Talan stared in horror at the bound and hooded Rees stretched out on Lady Pet's cool, tiled entrance hall.

Behind her, a fountain trickled, belying the heat and dust of the outer world. On the stairs beyond that, Lady Pet watched, interested.

"He didn't want to come," the bodyguard said defensively.

Talan swung around and glared at Lady Pet.

"It's no use looking at me," her foster mother said. "It took me forever to find him, and I told them under no circumstances was he to get away. I suppose they took me literally."

Talan made an exasperated noise and hurried down the stairs to the recumbent figure. He was still out.

Talan gently loosened the black silk hood and drew it off over his head.

Dust creased Rees' face. His dark blond hair was pulled back from his face, like before. His eyes were closed, and dark blond lashes lay against his cheeks.

His mouth was a pale line above a square jaw. She had an irresistible urge to kiss it.

"Rees," she whispered. She touched his cheek.

His eyes moved behind his eyelids. He made a faint moan, then he opened his eyes.

"Rees, it's me. Remember me? From the holo-block?"

Rees looked at her, and his eyes focused. "Talan."

His voice was as smooth and seductive as she remembered. The two syllables of her name never sounded so enticing.

Rees had blue eyes. *Shareem-blue*, Lady Ursula's diary called it.

29

The irises were larger than a normal humans' and flecked with black. When a Shareem was aroused, the irises expanded. They could fill almost their entire eyes with mesmerizing blue.

Rees' eyes drew her gaze, now, as they had in the holo-block. They said, *you're beautiful.*

His hands were still bound. "This could be fun if all these people weren't here," he murmured to her.

"I'm sorry," Talan said. "They had no right to do that to you."

He stared as though she was insane.

Lady Pet said, "You don't apologize to Shareem, Talan. You want one, he comes. That is what they have to do."

"You could at least be polite."

Rees looked like he was trying not to laugh.

"Rees, would you like to be a guest in my house?" Talan asked him.

"He doesn't have a choice, Talan," Lady Pet said.

Rees looked around him at the vaulted ceiling and paintings around the skylights, at the marble stairs Lady Pet stood on.

"I have a choice," he said. He looked back at Talan. "I'll stay."

Chapter Three

๊ฌ

In the year 3509, the company called DNAmo invented the men of the Shareem.

They were taller than conventional men. They were strong, blue-eyed, long-cocked, tight-assed. They knew how to bring a woman to ecstasy and exactly how to keep her there.

They were sought after by rich women who wanted wildness in the bedroom.

The Shareem were DNAmo's biggest success. They were also its downfall.

The Shareem were trained in every sexual art known to man, and woman. They were offered in one of three levels — pure sensual pleasure, games and wicked fun, or the ultimate barbarian...complete with whip.

A Shareem could entrance and mesmerize a woman with his voice and his touch. He could flood the air with endorphins and pheromones designed to make a woman melt as his feet.

Women adored them. Women desired them. And eventually, they feared them.

At one time, men ruled the world of Bor Narga. Legend went that when the planet was first colonized two thousand years earlier, the colonists were cut off from the mother planet for a hundred years by a solar storm and eventually abandoned.

The men, who had qualified to be colonists because of their strength, resilience, and survival skills, had risen to dominate. The women, who'd had equality on the mother planet, eventually succumbed to subservience.

On Bor Narga, strength meant survival. If a woman was not strong enough to survive on her own, she served a man who was.

Eventually, as the centuries passed and basic survival was assured, culture resumed. Women were beautiful adornments and served men on their knees.

In the year 2834, the war to end all wars killed most of the male population. By this time Bor Narga had become a planet to be reckoned with—it had wealth, weaponry, science, art.

Bor Narga won the war, but at a brutal cost of life. Women were forced to come out from behind their robes and take the jobs the men had left behind.

Then they discovered they were good at it.

Now men wrote poetry and made art, the practices of a world in which a large leisure class dominated. Women ran the government, commerce, and universities.

And indulged themselves with the Shareem.

Level ones made women feel good. Level twos made them laugh and blush when they remembered the games. Level threes touched a basic instinct they didn't want to talk about.

Then DNAmo, flushed with success, made Rees.

They didn't call him Rees. They called him R294E8S. Only Rees called himself Rees.

The news of the new Shareem leaked and suddenly every DNA company tried to get their hands on the secret of R294E8S.

DNAmo did experiments with R294E8S. They wanted to learn exactly what he could and would do.

The researchers, mostly women, found out the hard way what he could do and what he would do—to them. A researcher who volunteered to enter a room alone with Rees was both pitied and envied. He taught them how to fear him.

The researchers worried about what they'd done. They destroyed their notes. They talked about terminating him.

Then Rees disappeared.

DNAmo, after a long, tense, secret search, figured he was dead. Or off-planet. No longer their problem.

Soon after, the government of Bor Narga banned the breeding of Shareem, and DNAmo was forced out of business.

The Shareem, created from a pool of genetic material, made for sex alone, became taboo. DNAmo turned them out to fend for themselves.

A few of them were rumored to have gone underground, to live like kings with women to adore them. A few were rumored to have left the planet, though that had been forbidden.

Rees lived on his own and got by.

Everyone forgot about R294E8S.

Except Rees.

* * * * *

A few hours after his arrival at Talan's home, Rees, clad only in his loincloth, faced Lady Petronella alone in her sitting room. She'd asked to speak to him.

Rees could have gone home. As he'd told Talan, Shareem weren't slaves.

He definitely would have walked if anyone but Talan had pulled off the hood. But her blue eyes had held concern, and she'd looked so damn fuckable.

Anyone else, and he'd have gone. For Talan, he stayed.

Once the bodyguards had released Rees' hands, a neat, bearded man called Metri had taken him to a sumptuous bathroom.

The room was laid out like a bubbling stream in a woods. Water poured through rocks on its way to a deep pool.

Greenery and holo-walls gave him the feeling of bathing in a cool paradise, although the cheeping birds got on his nerves a little.

While he prepared himself, Rees fantasized about laying Talan down in the rushing water. He'd open her legs, show her how the water could pleasure her. He filed that thought away for future use.

He'd put a call through to Rio from the terminal in the bathroom. Rio had snarled at him, but promised to lay low until Rees contacted him again. The freighter pilot had been iffy, anyway.

Now Rees faced Lady Pet, wondering what she wanted to say. He was washed, oiled, inoculated. Ready.

"Talan is my foster daughter," Lady Pet began. "But I love her like a daughter. I found her abandoned when she was barely six months old."

Rees folded his arms, waited to hear Talan's life story.

"I took her in," Lady Pet went on. "The poor mite was starving. I had her DNA scanned, discovered she was high-born and who her parents were. They had been killed by the detox virus—I don't know if you remember, but it manifested on a starship and wiped out all aboard. The military decided to blow up the starship, so even if there were survivors... Anyway, I suppose whoever was designated to care for the baby no longer wanted to, and left her in a children's refuge. I saw her when I was there doing charity work, poor thing. I never had children of my own, and Talan has become dear to me. She is celibate, you know."

Rees nodded. "She wears the garb."

"Yes." Lady Pet's look turned long-suffering. "She is quite proud of it. The gods only know why. I sent her to the best schools, but she only learned how to be frigid. That is the way things are in our *enlightened* society today."

Yeah, these kids, Rees thought. *Not out screwing and rolling around like in the old days.*

"Talan has chosen celibacy," Lady Pet said, "but she explained to me that she wants to see what she might be missing."

Rees grinned. "Like a research experiment."

Rees already had a glimpse of how Talan's mind worked. And he was used to being a research experiment.

"Exactly. But I don't want you to be a specimen for her. I want you to turn the tables on her and show her precisely what it is she's giving up. I want her to fully understand what her body is made for. She deserves to know."

Rees nodded. "You want me to screw her so good she'll never want to be without it."

"I want you to make her know what it is to feel good. Those philosophers she worships try to make her ashamed she has breasts."

Rees rubbed his fingers over his oiled biceps, catching on the thin black chain. "I might be able to fix that."

Lady Pet's smile widened. "I trust you will. Go with Metri. He will show you the chamber I want you to use. I will send Talan there."

The door behind him whooshed open, wafting a draft of air over his naked flesh.

He turned and followed the majordomo from the room.

As they walked through the cool corridors, Rees wondered what Metri thought of Lady Petronella abducting him to pleasure Talan. The man wore a resigned look, as though thinking, *women will be women*.

The room Metri led him to was not the bathroom, but another holo-room. This one was blank when they entered. Metri showed him the panel from which Rees could select one of five choices.

He could choose woods with a gentle waterfall, the corner of an intimate restaurant, a flower garden with trickling fountains, a terrace overlooking a mountain lake, or a cabin that looked out to gently falling snow.

Because Bor Narga was a desert planet, most people ordered scenes that were cool, although the snow-covered trees made Rees a little too chilly. He didn't want Talan getting cold.

When Metri departed, Rees chose the woods. The air was cool and slightly damp from a trickling waterfall.

On a "tree" he found a hook, from which hung a pair of handcuffs. He smiled. Lady Petronella was thorough.

He could chain Talan up, gently strip off her clothes, run his tongue all over her body, including the breasts her philosophers wanted her to be ashamed of.

He wondered what she'd taste like. His cock was already hard.

The door whispered open again. He turned, his heart beating faster.

Talan had removed her outer three layers of robes and stood in a sleeveless gown tied at the waist. It was made of sun-blocking material, quite thick, but still outlined her curves. Her red hair hung in waves down her back.

Her arms were a little plump, and she probably wouldn't understand why he thought that was beautiful.

"Close the door," he said.

She closed it. "You understand why I asked Lady Petronella to find you."

"She told me." *Come a little closer, sweetheart.*

She took a step forward. "I chose you because I'd met you, and you seemed kind. Maybe that's why. Or maybe it was your pheromone trick."

Closer than that, babe. "That only works for a certain distance. It wears off when you leave. It's not a love spell."

She took another step. "Are you a level one Shareem?"

"No."

"Level two is games, is that right?"

"Yes."

"I don't know much about games," she said.

"Don't worry, I'll teach you." *Almost there, sweetheart.*

She took a third step, and then got bold and took a fourth. "I just want you to understand—"

Rees smiled. "Thank you."

He could move fast. He seized her by the wrists and had her hands pinned above her head before she could gasp out a question.

He closed the handcuffs around her wrists, and there she was, arms high, breasts outthrust, lips moist and parted.

He leaned down and licked those lips from end to end. They tasted wonderful.

Here's where the fun begins.

Talan's heart beat fast and hard. Her lips burned where his tongue had stroked them.

Her arms were stretched overhead, not too high, but she could not get loose.

"Why did you do that?" she ventured.

He leaned close. "So you won't run away."

He smelled good from his bath. His blond hair was dark and still sleek with water.

"I won't run away," she said.

"I don't believe you."

Would she run if he freed her this minute? She didn't think so. She stood rooted to the spot, she would probably stand with her hands over her head even if he took the cuffs away.

Her thighs were already creamy wet. If she ran away, it wouldn't help. She'd have to touch herself for release, like she'd read about in Lady Ursula's diary.

She imagined her fingers sinking into her slick, wet folds. She let out a gasp.

His body pressed hers to the holo-tree. His skin was hot and smelled like soap. "What are you thinking about?"

"Touching," she murmured.

"Touching what?"

"Me. My…"

"Your what?"

"My clit," she said hurriedly.

"Your pussy," he finished, his lips next to her cheek. His eyelashes flicked down. "Say it."

She swallowed, closing her eyes. She could shut out his face, and his pale lips so close to hers, but she couldn't shut out his body. It was hard, warm, and she wanted so much to kiss it.

"Say it," he repeated.

Talan said the words in a rush. "My pussy."

"Your sweet, creamy pussy."

She gulped. "My sweet, creamy pussy."

"Which is all wet with come for me?"

"Yes, I believe it is."

To her surprise, he chuckled. She opened her eyes. He had a wicked smile. It was warm, not cold or cruel. She liked looking at it. She tried a tiny smile back.

His expression changed. He took a step back, removed his loincloth, and tossed it aside.

She'd never seen a man's backside until she'd seen his. She'd never seen the front of a man, either.

Until now. His cock was *huge*. It stood straight out from his loins, the head engorged and full. A ridge ran around the tip where it met the rest of the shaft.

She had a sudden, overpowering urge to touch it, to see what it felt like. She strained against her bonds.

He closed his own hand around the cock. "It wants you," he said.

I want it. The thought shot through her before she could stop it. Her groin burned. A celibate woman of the Way should not think these things, should not feel anything.

Well, she was now.

"Tell me about the levels, again," she babbled. "What do they really mean?"

Rees ran his thumb around the tip of his cock. "Level one is sensuality. Everything sensual, like the feel of cloth or a chain on your skin. Or the feel of me inside you, full and tight."

Talan's already hot opening began to expand. It wanted him all the way, wanted to pull him in and keep him there. "And level two?"

"Games. Like putting you in handcuffs. Teasing you until you come, then backing off. Driving you crazy."

He would do it. He was looking forward to it.

"And…level three?"

"Nothing you are ready for."

She shivered. "I am not even ready for this."

"Yes, you are."

"How do you know?"

"I can sense it. The air is thick with your pheromones. That's you wanting me. That's how I know you're ready."

In a quick move, he untied the belt at her waist, dropped it to the floor. He unhooked the clasps that held her dress in place at her shoulders. She could only watch, helpless to prevent him.

She didn't want to prevent him. She suddenly wanted the dress off, wanted his hands on her body.

The gown puddled at her feet. Beneath it she wore a shift—sheer, white and silky. She'd always loved it, the only sexy thing she allowed herself. The cloth made her feel like she was being caressed.

"You have beautiful breasts," he said. He pinched one nipple, pulled it toward him. "Nice and full," he said. "I'm going to suck them raw."

Was it hard to breathe in here? "Then you will remove my hymen?"

He stopped. "What?"

"I am scheduled to go to the Ministry of Families clinic in a few weeks. To have my hymen removed. After I take the classes. But if you remove it, I'll have to cancel the appointment."

He stared at her. "Remove?"

"Yes."

"That means you still have it?"

"Yes."

His eyes took on a faraway look. "Mmm. A cherry-flavored pussy."

"Are you qualified to remove it?"

He leaned down, put his hands on either side of her. "Yes, Talan, I'm qualified to remove it."

"Are you going to do it now?"

Her body flushed. She knew he would break her hymen by driving his long cock into her. The head would penetrate it, flesh against flesh.

The Way of the Star was having a hard fight against his Shareem-touch and the chemicals he sent into her brain.

"I want you to do it now," she heard herself whisper.

"Good," he said.

He went back to caressing her breasts. Her nipples rose, tingling and hot. He licked her again, tracing his tongue across her jawline.

"When will you do it?" she asked.

He laced his hand through her hair, pulled her head back. "When I am ready."

His rock-hard cock rested against her belly. "But you are ready, now," she said.

He smiled. "Understand something, sweetheart. No matter how much you demand, no matter how much you beg, I'll fuck you when I want to. All right?"

His breath was spicy and scorching hot. She shook all over. "Yes. All right. I do beg your pardon."

He gave her another peculiar look. "I can't do this if you're going to make me laugh every five minutes."

She stared. "Why should I make you laugh?"

He looked her up and down, tapped his lips. "I see we're going to have to start from the very beginning."

"I am sorry. I've never had any training in this."

He smiled. "Gods, you're priceless." He did not sound displeased, just amused.

"The Ministry does not offer classes in this area," she explained.

He traced her cheek, his touch gentle. "There's more to life than classes, Talan. But don't worry, I'll be your teacher." He looked away, his gaze remote. "Thank gods you didn't see Rio first," he murmured.

"Rio? Who is Rio?"

Rees flicked his attention back to her. "A friend of mine. A level three."

"Will you tell me about level three someday?"

"I'll tell you. I might even introduce you to him." He stepped close to her again. "But not now. Now you need to learn level one."

Her heart quickened. "Sensuality."

"Sensuality." He nibbled her earlobe. "You like classes, so this will be your classroom. I'm the teacher. You have to do whatever I say, do you understand?"

She nodded. "I think so."

"When I ask you to do something, you say, 'yes, teacher'."

"All right."

He cocked a brow at her. Her lips formed the words, "Yes, teacher."

"Good." He skimmed his lips across her brow. "I think a girl in this room wants to be fucked. What do you think?"

"Yes, teacher."

"I think she wants to be paddled, and then fucked."

She started. "What?"

Rees raised his head, smiled. "Sorry, that's level two." He slid his hands around her waist, his palms warm through the silk. "Back to level one."

She shuddered. Level one was already driving her insane. She wanted him. She wanted him bad, no matter what the Way of the Star said. And he wasn't going to let her have him. It wasn't fair.

He leaned down and twirled his tongue over her breast through the silk. Her heart beat hard, and she was filled with sensations she'd never known. "It feels good."

"Does it, baby?" he murmured.

"Yes. Yes, it feels good."

"Yes, what?"

She gulped. "Yes, teacher."

He whispered something against her, then went on stroking her with his tongue. His eyes were closed, his mouth moving as he sucked her through her shift.

I'm going to suck you raw. The words should frighten her. Why did they excite her?

She moaned, arched back to send her breast deeper into his mouth.

"That's it, baby."

His eyes were heavy, his face flushed. He moved both his hands to her waist, caressing the curve of it, then moved to her buttocks. His hands were warm as he stroked her through the silk. "And what's this?"

"My posterior," she said.

He chuckled. "Your sweet ass."

She took hold of her courage. "My sweet ass."

His eyes flared. "That's a good girl." His hands moved in slow motion. "Your ass that I want to paddle. I really want to. But I won't. Not yet."

Her belly tightened as she thought about it.

He pressed a finger into the cleft of her buttocks through the cloth. He smoothed all the way down, pushing the silk a tiny way into her hole. "I'm going to go here one day. With my finger and my tongue."

"Really?"

"Yes, really. And my cock. Would you like my cock in your ass?"

She swallowed. "I don't know. Is that level one?"

"Baby, you keep making me laugh. No, not level one. But I want to do it anyway."

She shivered all over.

"Am I scaring you, sweetheart?"

He pulled her against him. She rested her head against his hard shoulder, wishing she could pull from the manacles and hold him. "A little," she answered.

"Shh," he said into her hair. "There's nothing to be afraid of. It will be pleasure, pure and simple. It's what I'm made for."

She leaned against him, loving his smell, the feel of his bare skin under her cheek. She could hear his heartbeat—thump, thump, thump—fast and excited. His skin was hot, damp with perspiration, even though the room was temperature-controlled.

To be close to him, she loved it. If only they could just do this…

"Why did you decide to stay, today?" she asked.

"Hmm? Because when I saw you before, I thought you were beautiful."

"In the holo-block."

"In the holo-block. I wanted to plow you so bad, baby."

She remembered the low velvet of his voice, the silken sound of his vowels as he'd asked her to stay with him that day.

"Why did you want me?" she asked.

"Because you're beautiful."

"I'm not beautiful. I'm…chubby."

"You're perfect."

Not according to Lady Pet, who kept encouraging surgery to get rid of her plumpness.

"Would you have done it, then?" she asked. "If I had asked you?"

"Probably," Rees murmured. "I wanted you so bad, little girl. I still do."

She leaned forward and kissed his collarbone. She felt his cock jump against her belly. "Is it different, now that you know why I want you?"

"Yes."

Disappointment pumped through her. "I wish…"

"You wish what?"

I wish it could be just you and me and nothing between us. I wish it could be real.

"I wish I wasn't so afraid," she finished.

"Don't be afraid, Talan."

She buried her face in his chest again. "When you talk to me like that, I'm not afraid."

"That's because my voice was made to soothe you." He looked down at her, eyes dark. "But you should be afraid of me, sweetheart. You should be afraid of all the things I want to do to you."

He'd just told her *not* to be afraid. "I don't understand —"

He slanted his mouth over hers, briefly. Her lips opened, wanted more.

"I'll do what you and your Lady Petronella want, teach you what it's like to be with a man." His eyes glittered. "But what I want to do, sweetheart—what *I* want to do…" He nipped her ear. "I want to fuck you every way there is to fuck you."

Her heart raced. "Do you? When will you?"

He straightened up, took his devastating touch away. "Not now. You've had enough now."

She cried out in disappointment. "No, I haven't. I haven't, really."

He gave her a severe look. "I said you've had enough. I am the teacher, you are the pupil. Right?"

"Yes, teacher."

He leaned over, picked up the loincloth he'd dropped. How he would fit it over his huge, hard cock, she didn't know.

He didn't try. "I'm going to release you, and I'm going to walk out of here. If you want satisfaction, you'll have to do it yourself. In fact, that's your homework. You aren't leaving this room until you've made yourself scream. All right?"

She stared at him, eyes wide. Her body crawled with need. "I —"

He came back to her, pinched her jaw between his thumb and fingers. "I said, all right?"

She gasped. "Yes. Teacher."

"Good. Now, goodnight."

He turned and strode away. She watched his ass, so tight and fine, his tapering back, his wide, strong shoulders.

Now that he'd stopped talking, the room was too quiet. The soft trickle of the water and the artificial breeze in the trees would never be as soothing as his dark voice.

When he reached the door, he lifted a remote from a shelf near it. She thought it was for the holo, but when he pressed it, her manacles suddenly released.

Her arms dropped, half-painful, half-tingling. She stood there, rubbing her wrists.

"Make yourself scream, Talan," he instructed.

He opened the door, blew her a kiss, and walked out of the room. Stark naked. Metri would faint.

The door closed, and Talan was left alone.

She throbbed with need, whimpering with it. He'd opened something inside her, stirred fires she never knew she had.

She fell to her knees on the damp holo-earthen ground. She could only think of his hands on her, his mouth on her, his voice telling her to say things she'd never have dreamed of saying.

She slid her hand between her thighs to cup her groin. She was slick and hot, and her fingers went willingly into her opening.

She wasn't sure what to do, but she started to rub, and rub, and so began her release.

Chapter Four

ფ

Rees reached the bedchamber they'd told him was his without meeting anyone. Lady Pet must have told the servants to keep clear.

The chamber was plain, though comfortable, the bedroom of a servant. He had a bed, a closet for his belongings, and a monitor. A tiny adjoining room contained the necessaries.

It wasn't much, but still better than what they'd given him at DNAmo.

They'd been afraid of him at DNAmo.

He entered the room, tossed his loincloth to the bunk, and tried to tell his cock to calm down.

It didn't listen.

Gods, he needed that girl. He needed to bury himself inside her and come and come and come.

He balled his fists. His cock was acting like one of those magic swords of legend that had to taste battle before it could be sheathed. It told him it had to taste her pussy before he could put it away again.

He wrapped his hand around it. It throbbed and jerked, wanting her.

He remembered running his hands over her warm body through the silk, the brief, tantalizing taste of her tongue, the longing he could smell and feel in the air.

If you want satisfaction, you'll have to do it yourself, he'd told her, trying to act like he didn't care.

He'd give anything to run back, spread her legs, find her release for her.

She would be in there, alone, her hands filled with cream, shaking and sobbing as she touched herself.

He looked at the monitor. He remembered seeing a small round lens near the ceiling of the holo-room. Security, he'd thought.

He found the remote, switched on the monitor. Playing a little, he found the frequency of cameras inside the house. He found the one in the holo-room.

Talan was still there.

She knelt on the floor, her silk shift hiked above her hips, her lovely red hair falling past her shoulders. Her eyes were closed. Her lips had parted, her chest lifting with her rapid breath.

She stroked her right hand over her pussy, moaning with the pleasure of it. Her fingers gleamed.

Look at all that come. Sweet little girl, I want to taste that.

He imagined his tongue between her thighs, cream filling his mouth. His hand moved on his cock.

Yes, baby, stroke it hard.

Her left hand played with her breasts through the silk, fumbling a little, as though she didn't know how.

"Go on, baby," he said to the monitor.

As though she heard him, she rubbed faster. Her little cries increased.

Rees rubbed his cock. It tingled and throbbed. "Cream for me, baby. My cock is jumping for you."

She went on and on. He found out he could zoom in on her. He focused on her hand, watched her push her fingers inside, watched her hips buck as she did.

"That's my cock, Talan. My cock in you, so hard."

He imagined it, her hot folds squeezing him tight. She was a virgin. She'd be so tight, as tight as her ass.

She started to scream. It startled her, her eyes flew open. She shoved both hands hard against her groin, keeping up the agonizing strokes on her clit. Her hips moved, little female noises escaped her mouth.

In his room, Rees also came. He imagined squirting high inside her. His own hips moved, as though she was wrapped around him.

He licked his shoulder, tasting his hot skin and wishing it were her.

In the holo-room, Talan lay on the earth floor, her hair damp with humidity and sweat, her hand still pressed to her clit.

She was quieting now, her gasps winding down into little sighs. She lay there, a small smile on her face, her eyes aglow with wonder.

Gods, he wished he could be holding her in his arms right now. She'd kiss him gently, wrap her arms around him, hold him close.

He had not needed to leave her, but his nature had wanted to torture her a little.

So who's being tortured here?

Shaking like he never had before, he pressed a kiss to his fingertips, then touched them to the screen.

In the morning, Rees found the garden. A real one. He reached it through a maze of hallways, passing through an unmarked door.

Holo-outdoor scenes looked and felt real, but they could never be perfect. The shadows would be wrong or the water not quite right or the sand the wrong temperature.

But this was completely real. Trees grew along a fence line, blocking the garden from the reality of the harsh street. A canopy of shade cut off the heat of the sun, the cool scent of rich earth and grass pervaded. Roses twined through a trellis and climbed the trees, their red and yellow blossoms lending perfume to the air.

Rees stared in wonder. He'd never seen a real garden before. He wondered how they kept out the desert sands, until he watched an insect bounce off an invisible field far above.

What must it be like to have so much money you could have a permanent garden? Not only did Talan live in a huge, mazelike house with every comfort, but she could go outside and still have the heat and sands kept at bay.

This was how Talan had grown up. Privileged, pampered, her every need met. And yet she was not spoiled or grasping, as she could have been.

She was sweet as spring sunshine. Her skin was a joy to touch, her cries the most exciting sounds he'd ever heard.

He grinned. Listen to him being poetic. Rio would die laughing.

Rees walked across the leaf-strewn path to the opposite door, reveling in the cool joy of the garden. No sign or force field had forbidden him to walk there, so he assumed it was open to anyone in the house.

The door on the other side led to a dining room. The room had a clear glass wall so that those inside could look out to the pretty garden. The door stood open.

The people in the dining room, Metri and Talan, did not see him approach. They were too busy arguing.

"There is no reason why he cannot take meals with us, Metri," Talan was saying. "Why should he eat with the servants? He is not a servant, any more than you are."

Metri turned bright red behind his beard. It must have rankled to be put in the same category as one of the Shareem. "Lady Petronella does not wish it."

"Did she say she did not wish it?"

"Not in so many words. But Shareem do not share a table with high-born ladies. It isn't done."

"High-born ladies should not even speak to them. Are we to be hypocrites then, and pretend he isn't here?"

Metri looked exasperated. *Poor man.*

Rees entered the dining room. Metri's bearing became stiff.

"I heard," Rees said. "Your majordomo is right, Talan. Shareem should not share tables with high-born ladies."

Talan's face blossomed bright pink. Her eyes went all starry when she did that. He remembered the feel of her skin beneath his hands, the salty taste of her lips. She had a great capacity for pleasure. He had barely tapped it.

"Ridiculous," Talan said breathlessly. "Sit next to me, Rees."

Sweet girl. Was she being generous, or trying to put one over on her guardian's majordomo?

"Please," she said. She slid out the chair next to her, patted it.

Rees winked at her, shot an apologetic grin at Metri, and sat down.

At least Metri did not have to worry about Rees being naked. Rees had found, when he'd risen and washed, a clean, insulated tunic and dark blue outer robe with a finely woven belt. He'd donned all this, thinking that living like a rich boy wasn't such a bad thing.

The food was already on the table, kept warm or cool in its own programmed dish. Talan nibbled on a piece of bright orange hothouse fruit. Her soft lips closed around it, as she gently sucked.

He watched her a minute, enjoying it.

Then he piled his own bowl with fruit and covered it with cream. Her pheromones were thick in the air. That and watching her suck on the fruit made his already stiff cock throb even harder.

She was driving him crazy.

But it wasn't just her pheromones. It was *her*. When he'd watched her in the monitor last night, not one pheromone had reached him in his remote part of the house. He'd gotten off just watching her stroke herself and come for him.

The fruit and cream gave him good ideas, too.

Metri left the room. Probably to lie down and get over his shock of a Shareem in the dining room.

"Did you sleep well?" Talan asked Rees.

Rees took a bite of fruit. The juices filled his mouth. "Not really."

"Why not?" She looked concerned. "Was the bed uncomfortable? The room too hot? I told Metri to adjust the temperature—"

"The room is fine. I spent the night thinking how much better the bed would be with you in it."

Her face went rosy.

Why had he said that? He was here to train her, to rid her of her fears about sex. Not to blather like an adolescent about how much he wanted her.

The situation was deteriorating fast. He should leave.

But if he left, Talan would simply hire another Shareem. That Shareem would touch her, would teach her...

No! came the explosive thought. *Mine.*

He heard sardonic laughter in the back of his mind. *Yours? You are Rees. If you really want to be nice to this woman, you'll walk out this morning and leave her alone.*

Fuck that.

"I did what you told me," Talan said shyly.

Rees dipped a hothouse strawberry in the thick cream, popped it in his mouth. "What was that?"

"I touched myself." She closed her eyes, drew a breath that raised her chest against her thick garments. "I've never felt anything like that before."

"I know. I saw you."

Her eyes widened. "You saw me?"

"In the monitor. I watched you." He chewed the strawberry, swallowed. "You were a good girl. I won't have to punish you. Not yet."

Her mouth became a round, pink "o".

Down boy, said the voice inside him. *Stick to level one.*

"What do you want to do this morning?" he asked her, trying to make his voice normal.

"Lady Pet has gone out to shop," she answered, a little breathlessly. "I thought I would study."

"A good idea. Yes, let's study."

She blushed. "I mean my texts. Philosophy."

"Mmm. Sounds boring."

"Oh, no, it's quite interesting. About how to free your mind from the body and become purely intellect. No emotions, no feelings to drag you down."

He took another bite of fruit, enjoyed the bright taste of it. "But your mind is always connected to your body," he said. "Unless you cut off your head."

"Don't be silly. You have no idea of the freedom and bliss that comes with following the pure intellect."

He looked at her narrowly. "Is the bliss anything like what you felt last night?"

She blushed. "That was different. I have not yet learned the discipline to pull away from my body. That is one reason I wanted to bring you here. To learn to resist. I want the discipline. I don't want—" She broke off, looked embarrassed.

"To be like me?" Rees shook his head. "Talan, you'll never be able to separate your intellect from your body. You have to learn to enjoy your body, learn to live in it every moment. Not become separated from it."

"You are Shareem. You say that because that is how they train you."

"I didn't learn that growing up at DNAmo. What I know I learned from surviving. I've learned to listen to my body, but not let it dictate my life." *At least, not until now,* the voice mocked. "But if I'd tried to separate my thoughts from my body, I'd be dead."

She looked puzzled. "You grew up there? But DNAmo went out of business twenty years ago."

"Shareem age slowly," Rees explained. Especially R294E8S. That had been one of the experiments, to expand his life, slow down the aging process, even more than on most Shareem.

Her eyes filled with curiosity. She opened her mouth to ask more, but suddenly the pressure in the house changed.

The morning sunshine vanished, blotted out by a thick yellow cloud that struck the house full force.

For a moment, Rees felt like someone was pressing an invisible weight on the top of his head. Then the fields protecting the house adjusted to the change in air pressure, and the feeling went away.

"Sandstorm," Talan said worriedly. "It was not supposed to hit until this afternoon."

Rees marveled at the calm way the household took the arrival of the deadly storm. Down in Pas City, where Rio lived and Judith had her bar, they would shut down all the doors, sit against the walls, and wrap cloths over their faces until the storm passed.

Everyone let anyone in off the streets when a sandstorm hit. It was an unwritten rule.

Here, the house went on as usual. The slight pressure change was the only acknowledgement that a deadly storm raged outside.

Talan, a worried look on her face, rose from the table and pressed a button to call Metri. He scuttled in after only a few moments.

"Lady Petronella is out," she said. "Is she all right?"

Metri nodded, making a reassuring gesture. "She is at the house of Lady Mira. She called not five minutes ago to tell me. She is fine."

Talan looked relieved and dismissed the majordomo.

She cared, Rees realized. Lady Pet was an odd sort of woman to be Talan's guardian, and their thinking was at odds, but Talan cared for her. So much so, that her first thought upon beholding the sandstorm was concern for Lady Pet's safety.

He wondered what it would feel like to have her concerned for him.

This was getting out of hand.

He snatched up the bowls of cream and golden fruit. "Time for lessons, Talan," he said, then walked away from her and back to the garden.

Chapter Five

ဢ

Talan followed him into the garden, her intellect losing the battle to her curiosity.

The sandstorm thrashed and grated against the field far above, but it could not penetrate the force screen. The screen was powered by a class five generator, the best made. So while the storm raged in the streets, this garden remained cool and peaceful.

Talan felt anything but peaceful. He'd angered her with his dismissal of her philosophy, but she should feel sorry for him, really.

It was not his fault that his genes had been manipulated, his DNA code changed so that he could never achieve the philosophical freedom that she could. He would be forever tied to his body. She should feel superior.

Instead, she wanted to run after him and apologize for arguing. She had the most absurd urge to please him.

Lady Pet would scoff that Talan had an absurd urge to please everyone, but this was different. Talan pleased others because it was her duty, because she wanted to show that she had manners.

She wanted to please Rees because she *wanted* to. She wanted him to look at her with that sparkle in his blue eyes and tell her he liked her pleasing him.

She knew he'd been made to make her want to please him. She had read all about DNAmo and the Shareem after she'd found Lady Ursula's diary. She had learned disturbing things.

A Shareem could modulate his voice to the most pleasing pitch to a woman's ears. Rees could taste her pheromones on the air, he could project his own to excite her, or project endorphins to make her feel relaxed and soothed.

He could not actually force her to feel anything she did not want to, but he could manipulate conditions so that she'd most likely feel what he wanted.

This was how Shareem had serviced their decadent women in the past. They'd been created to please, but the women had begun to want more than simple pleasure.

They'd grown bored and made their Shareem into more and more wicked creatures, willing and ready to do anything to extend the game of desire.

The things Talan had read about the level three Shareem had shocked her. Rees, she thought after what they'd done yesterday, must be level two.

Even level twos had been shocking, but level threes had gone into the realm of things she'd never known existed.

When DNAmo had closed and departed, people talked about what to do with the Shareem. Some had argued that they weren't truly human. They did not have parents—they'd been grown in a jar filled with the best DNA available.

A contingent had wanted to kill them. Not in a brutal way, they'd said hastily. Give them injections that would kill them instantly and cremate the bodies. End of problem.

But many stockholders, already upset at their declining returns, had thought that too inhumane. The vote had been close, but the Shareem had been allowed to live—if they agreed to follow stringent rules and stay away from decent society, of course.

And Talan had brought one into her house.

Rees stared at the sandstorm high above them. "Does the field ever break?" he asked.

Talan shook her head. "Lady Pet keeps everything in good repair."

He continued to stare upward, the muscles of his neck tight. "Oh well, danger always adds spice."

A vicious sandstorm could strip a woman's flesh from her bones. The bursts of wind sent rock and sand against buildings and humans like a grinding machine. It would kill a person not protected by thick clothing and a breath mask.

Talan had never been anything but safe from the storms. The storm watchers always gave fair warning, and it was a rare person who got caught in them. Today, however, it had blown in unexpectedly early.

"What are we going to do?" she asked Rees.

He set the bowls of fruit and cream on a wooden table next to a garden bench. "Tell Metri and the rest of your staff to stay away."

Talan pressed a keypad outside the door. All the windows and the glass wall of the dining room went dark. "They will only come if I call."

"Well, you might be screaming pretty loud." He winked. "At least, I hope so."

A shiver went down her spine. How could he make what should be frightening seem so desirable?

Because he's trained to, she reminded herself. *That voice makes you want to do anything he says.*

Rees stripped off his robe. Beneath it, he wore a sleeveless linen tunic. His hard body filled it out, and the black chain around his biceps gleamed.

He lifted a piece of bright orange fruit in his fingers. "What is this?"

"Mango."

He dipped it into the bowl of cream. "It's good. Come here."

She went to him slowly, her heart beating hard. "Yes, teacher."

He gave her a hot look. "That was yesterday's game. Today, we will play something different."

"What will we play?"

"Do not ask so many questions. Or I *will* paddle you."

And why did her heart race every time he said *that*? She really needed to read more philosophy.

He held out the fruit to her. She reached for it.

He pulled it away. "Just eat it."

She understood. She leaned down and closed her lips over it.

He pressed the fruit into her mouth. The sweet juices spurted as she bit down.

"Mmm," she said. He slowly wiped his thumb across her lips, then he raised it to his own mouth and licked the leftover cream from it.

She silently chewed and swallowed the fruit.

His eyes went dark. He took her face between his hands and kissed her.

His mouth was warm, his lips strong. His tongue delved into her, stroking her. She slid her arms around his neck. This was what Lady Ursula had done with her Shareem. Woven tongues together and embraced in warmth.

She'd envied them.

She traced her fingers over Rees' back, loving every muscle, every strong sinew. His hands slid to her bottom, pulled her tight against him.

She moved her hips, wanting him to touch the hot ache of her clit. So far, only she had touched herself, he'd scarcely put his hands on her.

He kissed her cheekbone, traced her jaw with his tongue.

"Rees," she whispered.

He went on licking her, wetting her face, his tongue hot and possessive.

"Rees, I want you."

He licked his way down her throat. He began to bite then, sharp nips of her flesh. He shoved her hair out of his way, bit her neck, sucked, like a vampire. It hurt, and it was darkly erotic, and she loved it.

He kissed and bit across her shoulder. He hadn't asked her to take off her clothes. Had told her to stop asking questions.

"What do you want me to do?" she whispered. "I want to please you."

He bit her, hard. She gasped. He lifted his head. His eyes glittered, the blue filling the white. "*I* please *you*. That is why you brought me here."

She shook her head, feeling half-drunk. "You pleased me, yesterday. I want to please you, today."

Maybe he wanted her to play. He was a level two, maybe he wanted her to play a game. "What do you want me to do?" she whispered.

His eyes went hot. He put heavy hands on her shoulders. "Get on your knees."

Her legs went weak, and she shivered with excitement.

She found it easy to kneel before him. She saw the outline of his cock behind his tunic, right at her eye level. She licked her lips. She liked this game.

He lifted his tunic. His cock sprang out, big and hard and long. She liked looking at it. She could kneel here all afternoon and stare at it and be perfectly happy.

"Kiss it," he said.

She drew in a harsh breath. She fast approached realms she did not understand.

"Kiss it," he repeated. "Do what I say."

Talan leaned forward, pressed a kiss on the smooth, engorged head right in front of her.

His skin was smooth and so warm. It felt good to her lips and tasted salty. She kissed it twice more for good measure.

A bead of moisture welled up from the tiny slit in its center. She licked it off.

He tensed, the muscles of his thighs and abdomen tightening. "*Gods*, Talan."

"Is that what you want?"

He reached over to the table, came up with a handful of cream. He plopped it right onto his cock. "Suck it clean."

Talan smiled. She leaned forward again, licked a dab of cream from the tip.

His voice became harsh. "No, don't lick it. Suck it."

Talan screwed up her courage, opened her mouth, and wrapped her lips around the end of his cock.

It jumped in her mouth. She took the cream onto her tongue, swallowed. She sucked more. Another inch went inside. She kept sucking, tasting the tang of him and the mellowness of the cream. She nipped him, like he had done to her neck. He let out a groan.

Did I hurt you? she wanted to ask. But his hand went to her shoulder, gripped it fiercely. "That's it, Talan. Suck me, baby. Suck me hard."

She sucked. She wiped her tongue all over his head, tasting the difference between the smooth tip, the flange, the shaft.

She sucked some more, her lips hurting from stretching so far. But she did not want to stop.

He threaded his fingers through her hair, twisting it. "Gods, that's good."

She blindly touched the base of his shaft. Her hand met coarse, curled hair and scalding hot skin. He jumped.

"I'm going to come," he said hoarsely, his Shareem voice broken. "And you are going to swallow me down, Talan."

She was not certain what he meant. His hips moved, his hands in her hair tightened.

And then she felt her mouth fill with hot, salty liquid, burning her tongue and the back of her throat.

She jerked away in surprise. His hands shoved her back onto his cock, forcing her to take it, to let him fill her mouth.

"Swallow it, baby. Swallow it for me."

She drew back slowly, taking the liquid into her mouth, wrapping her tongue around the tip to get every drop. She swallowed it down, burning and hot all the way to her belly.

She looked up, licking her lips. "Was that right?"

He grabbed her shoulders and dragged her to her feet. He plunged his tongue inside her mouth, tasting himself on her tongue. He held her so tight, she could barely breathe. His cock, hardly less rigid than before, ground into her belly.

She twined her arms around him, reveling in how much he wanted her.

He seized her face between his palms. "I want to fuck you, baby. I want to fuck you and fuck you. I want to fill you full of me, then I want to put my come deep inside you. Do you understand me?"

"Yes." She wanted it too, so bad. A dim part of her knew he'd cast his Shareem spell on her, that she should not want this, but she told the dim part of her mind to go out and play in the sandstorm.

"I want to turn you over and come in your ass. The ass that I've paddled until it's red. Do you still understand me?"

"Yes."

His grip tightened. "I want you to beg for it. I want you to beg me to fuck you."

Her mouth was so dry, she couldn't form words. His eyes went dark, dangerous. "Beg me, Talan. Or I'll take your ass without preparing you, and that will hurt."

She gulped. "Please, Rees."

"Please what?"

"Please fuck me. Please fuck me, Rees."

"Beg me to fuck your sweet ass."

"Yes. Please, Rees, fuck my ass."

He stared at her, eyes boring into hers, a madness there she'd never seen in him before. The game had gone away, and she began to feel, through whatever he projected over her, a twinge of fear.

"You're a bad girl, Talan."

"I know. Please punish me. Please fuck me."

He drew a long, long breath. His hands on her face softened, the hard grip loosening.

"Gods, Talan," he whispered. "You're not ready. I don't want to hurt you, sweetheart."

"I want you to. It would be a good hurt. I want you to hurt me good."

He shook his head, his face against hers. "No, love. You're just feeling what I want you to feel. What I'm trained to make you feel."

"No," she whimpered.

"I'm afraid so, baby."

He gathered her close. She rested her head on his shoulder, his warmth soothing her. She shook all over, clutching at his tunic, which he hadn't taken off. Tears leaked from her eyes.

He was shaking, too. He, the trained Shareem, breathed fast, his heart pounding.

She did not understand what she was thinking, could not separate what she really felt with what he'd made her feel. "I want you, Rees."

"No, Talan. You're not ready."

She raised her head. His jaw was hard, sandpaper rough. "How do you know?"

"Because I am Shareem. I know when a woman's body is ready for what she desires and when it is too soon."

"When will I be ready? I want to be ready now."

He laughed softly, his velvet voice returning. "Not long."

She put her lips to his ear. "My cunt is all wet, Rees."

His laugh turned wicked. "I just bet it is."

"What do you want me to do? Do you want me to touch myself while you watch?"

"Hmm, that would be nice. But I have another idea."

He lifted the bowl of cream from the table. She smiled, her pulse still racing.

She was calming from the madness of a few minutes ago, when she'd wanted nothing more than for him to push her facedown onto the bench and shove his cock deep inside her. She'd wanted to take it and cram it in herself.

But the look on his face, the cream in his hands, started to be just as exciting.

"Sit on the bench," he said. "And spread your legs."

She started to comply. But just then, a tearing sound came from overhead, and in the next instant, the canopy faltered and the winds of the sandstorm came screaming in.

Talan gaped, and found her mouth and nose full of sand. The bowl of cream shattered to the floor.

She clutched at Rees. They needed to get into the house. She must lead him there, or he would die.

She could not find him in the yellow-brown mass. One moment he'd been standing next to her, the next, he was gone. She groped for him.

Suddenly a strong arm wrapped around her waist, lifted her from her feet. Rees took two steps, three, and then they were falling in through the open windows of the parlor.

Rees disentangled himself from her and slammed his hand against the window's panel.

The window sealed. Sand that had swirled in with them rained to the white carpet, then all was still.

The sandstorm, furious, beat at the windows, but could not get in.

Rees leaned against the wall, panting. Talan crawled up onto the sofa and lay there, shaken.

Metri and two footmen came scuttling into the room, eyes wide. "Are you all right?" Metri exclaimed.

"Fine," Talan croaked. "Rees got us out in time."

"But the garden is ruined," Rees said. He sounded morose. "That beautiful garden."

Metri looked at Rees as though reassessing him. "Lady Pet will have the garden repaired. But the two of you look awful. I suggest a bath."

Rees shot Talan a look. She knew she had sand all over her and must look a mess. Rees' hair had gone a shade darker, and sand had collected in the hollows under his eyes.

"A bath," he said, his voice still hoarse. "Good idea." He held out his hand. "Talan?"

And she, under Metri's stunned gaze, took Rees' hand and let him lead her out of the room.

Chapter Six

ও

"I really wanted to use the cream," Rees said as they entered the bathroom.

He still held Talan's hand and felt her trembling. That had been close.

Thank the gods he had noted the placement of the door and window control panels when they'd gone into the garden in the first place. He always took note of control panels in case a sudden storm blew in and he needed to get to the nearest shelter.

Talan hadn't known where to go. She'd been blundering into the middle of the garden when he'd caught her.

He watched Talan shake the sand out her skirts. The sandstorm had been a blessing in disguise, because Rees, in the garden, had lost control.

Shareem never lost control. *It's our gift*, Rio had said. Rio was always in control. Whenever Rees and Rio shared a lady, Rio was always master.

Rees let him for his own reasons. Rio decided whether he would watch while Rees fucked, or whether Rees would offer his cock to the lady's mouth while Rio took her from behind. Rio was always in charge.

No matter what they actually did, it was all about control. The lady in question surrendered control, which was what was so exciting about the Shareem. She surrendered herself to Rio and his exotic moods — or to Rees, who was unpredictable.

Rio always took control because he knew what would happen if Rees did.

In the garden, Rees had wanted Talan so bad, he'd have hurt her to get it. She'd gotten excited and started begging him, but that was just her biochemistry going crazy in reaction to his.

If the sandstorm had not pulled him back to sanity, Rees would have fucked her and fucked her, then put her under his arm and dragged her off home with him and kept her there.

His woman, to fuck when he wanted, kiss when he wanted, put his arms around when he wanted.

In the holo-block weeks ago, he'd wanted that too. He hadn't been simply reacting to her pheromones. He'd wanted *her*. He had to be insane.

Thank gods the sandstorm had hit.

Now he was back in control. This was his room, his job, his rules, no matter how much she smiled at him.

He locked the door, picked her up, and dumped her into the flowing stream.

She squealed. She scrambled up, lifting her dripping skirts. "My dress will get all wet."

He didn't laugh. "It's all sandy. What's the difference?"

"Don't you want me to take it off?"

"I want you to pull up your skirts and sit down."

She looked bewildered. "Why?"

"I told you not to ask questions. Obey me and sit down."

She smiled a little and plopped into the stream, her skirts above her hips.

His pulse sped. She sat square in the water, her sweet ass all wet and waiting for him.

He pulled his sand-ruined tunic from his body and tossed it on the floor. Naked, he straddled the stream, one foot on either side of it, and looked down at her. "It's too bad about the cream," he said softly. "But we don't really need it."

"I can send to the kitchens for more."

Gods, what a woman. "Shut up and spread your legs."

She did. She held the skirt bunched on her stomach. The water flowed past her legs, wetting her cunt. Droplets glittered like jewels in her red hair.

"You have a pretty pussy," he said softly. "Show me your pussy."

She did not know what to do. She lifted her hips a little, touched her clit.

"Show me," he purred. "Spread it out."

She put her fingers on either side of her opening, pulled it open. Sweet and pink and beckoning to him.

"Do you want me to lick you?" he asked.

Her eyes rounded, dark pools of blue in the shadows. "Yes. Please."

Much tamer, this. He put his feet in the water, enjoyed the cool flow over them. He knelt in front of her. He stroked one finger all the way down her opening.

She moaned. He put his finger in his mouth, sucked away the cream.

She tasted fine, like honey on a summer's day.

Poetry again. What was wrong with him?

He put his face down to her. She smelled good. He stroked his thumb along her clit, and then followed it with his tongue. She made a faint noise in her throat.

His control wavered for a split second before he regained it again. Sheesh, he was only licking her cunt.

He raised his head. "If you don't want me to do this, Talan, you have to say."

Her face flushed, her eyes closed. "I want it."

I want it, too. I want all of you.

And I can't ever have you. I'll take you as far as you need to go, and then I'll leave and never see you again.

It was enough to make a grown Shareem cry.

He lowered to her again, circled her clit with his tongue, tasting the spice of her. Then he slid his tongue into her opening.

She squirmed, making hot noises. Sweet cream touched his mouth. She was wet, oh, she was wet, she was loving this.

He licked and licked her. His tongue grew sore, and still he licked her. He traced her opening, thrust inside again.

Her hands tangled in his hair. She forgot to hold up the dress, and it fell over his face. Sand trickled into his mouth.

He turned aside, spat it out. Then he raised the dress himself, leaned down to her again.

"Rees," she whispered.

Rees.

Not a play name, not what he told her to say. Just her sweet voice calling his name.

His cock throbbed, hard. He wanted more than anything to push her back, slide right into her.

Not yet. Not yet. He was supposed to be slow and sensual, bringing her to complete readiness first. Then he'd take her slowly, teach her to want it, teach her how pleasurable it was to have a man inside her.

Control.

She leapt under his mouth. She was coming. His tongue was all wet with her, and she pulsed around him.

Now, now, now! Take her!

You are Rees. You can have whatever you want, and you know what you want.

Rees sank his fingers into her thighs, held himself in place. She bucked and rocked and screamed her pleasure.

Her pleasure. That's why he was here.

He sucked at her clit, driving her ever more wild. He drank her down, and then he sat back on his heels and licked it from his lips.

She lay down, her dress all wet, the water running between her legs. Her screams had wound down into breathy sighs, and her eyes were half-closed.

She was beautiful.

"You look sweet," he said, grinning.

"I do?"

"You're beautiful, Talan. Don't let anyone tell you different." He licked the last drop of her from his lips. "And you taste so good."

"I do?"

He laughed. "Better than anything I've ever tasted. Here."

He pulled her up into his arms and brought his mouth down on hers.

Her lips were soft, curious. They slid against his, and then, whether she meant to or not, opened for him.

He probed her tongue with his, then slanted his mouth over hers. The kiss grew deep. And dangerous.

Her tongue moved against his, unpracticed. He tasted her to the corners of her mouth, even as she tasted him.

He sank his hands into her hair.

He wanted her so bad. He wanted to slide into her and show her what it was like. He wanted her to beg, not because he told her to, but because she truly wanted him.

Women wanted Rees because he was Shareem. He wanted this woman to want Rees.

Take her, R294E8S said. *Let her scream. You'll have gotten what you came for.*

R294E8S could really be a bastard.

Rees eased the kiss to its end. She clung to him, her lips parted, her breath hot.

"Did you like it?" he asked.

She nodded. She twined her arms about his neck, brought him back down for another kiss.

He kept this one shorter, though it was just as heady.

"You have nice eyes," she whispered.

Rees, by the gods, felt himself blush. "Thank you."

"Can I suck you again? Like I did in the garden?" Her lashes swept down, and she looked coy. "Like a good girl?"

"You are learning, darling," Rees said. His cock throbbed so hard, he had to shove it somewhere before he died.

She got to her knees, holding her soaking dress. "Sit down," she said, a wicked glint in her eye. "And spread your legs."

He obeyed.

He came two more times in her mouth, he was so desperate, until Metri piped in a message to say that the sandstorm had gone.

* * * * *

Lady Petronella returned home safely, having waited out the sandstorm at the home of her friend. She summoned Talan to her as soon as she settled in her suite to repair her makeup.

"Well?" she said to the mirror. She'd dismissed the maid so that she and Talan could speak alone.

"Well, what?" Talan asked from the window.

She knew exactly what, but she pretended to watch the street and the park in the middle of the square. Work women and hovercraft had emerged to repair the damage from the storm, at the same time Lady Pet inspected damage to her face.

"Well, have you lost your fear of sex?"

"I never feared it," Talan answered. Below her, a woman in coveralls rose on a grav-free lift to trim a broken limb of a succulent tree. "I only said I did not wish it in my marriage."

"Well, the Shareem will not marry you. And I asked you if you liked it."

"It is not the same thing, is it?" Talan turned from the window. "He is trained to make me like it."

Lady Pet's gaze was intense. "So you do like it."

"So far." Her face grew hot. "He has not done much more than touch me."

That was true—in a technical sense. But what he'd said to her, what he'd made her feel, the wicked games he'd made her play, the phrases he wanted her to speak—

A dark feeling coiled in her belly.

Lady Pet looked surprised. "That is all? Metri said you were with him all morning. He has not even had intercourse with you?"

"Not yet."

"Why on earth not?"

Talan pressed her mouth shut. She did not want to discuss this with Lady Pet. Not only did it embarrass her, but she wanted to keep it private. Rees was hers.

Hers. Now where had that foolish idea come from?

"Talan," Lady Pet said. She turned in her chair, tapped her toe.

"He said I was not ready," Talan replied.

"Hmph. He's drawing it out so he can enjoy the luxury of my house."

"No, he is being kind. I am not ready."

She remembered herself in the garden, begging him to fuck her—in her behind, no less.

He'd told her that she did not mean that, that he'd cast his Shareem spell on her, but he was wrong. She'd wanted him, wanted him any way possible.

"Yes, well, I'll spare your delicate feelings for now. But if he does not hurry, I can always hire another. The back streets are thick with Shareem if you know where to look."

"*No.*"

Talan's answer rang loud in the room. Lady Pet's perfect brows arched.

"No," Talan repeated. "I know Rees now. I don't want anyone else."

Lady Pet looked at her for a long time, brows raised, her look interested. Then she shook her head and turned back to her mirror. "Very well. But he needs to finish. I do not like being taken advantage of."

Talan could bear no more. She walked stiffly to the door. Usually gentle-tempered, at that moment, she was very, very angry.

"It's nothing to do with you," she said in a hard voice.

Lady Pet stared at her in the mirror, then turned around as if she had not heard right.

Talan went on, "It is to do with me, and my life. Not you."

Lady Pet continued to stare. Talan closed her mouth. Breathing hard, she left the room.

She would not have been happy to see what Lady Petronella did after she marched away. Lady Pet turned back to the mirror and grinned at her reflection.

"About time that girl stood up to me," she said.

* * * * *

Rees chewed the last morsel of his apricot salad just as the door chime softly rang.

Everything in this house was quiet and polite. He punched the enter button and door slid open.

Talan stood framed in the doorway, her lovely red-gold hair covered with an opaque veil that hung down her back. Her gown, long-sleeved and hanging to her ankles, covered her completely, but the silk of it clung to her curves.

"Oh," she said, looking at his empty plate. "I was going to take you out to lunch."

A bite of disappointment surprised him. "Metri sent it. He thought I'd be hungry, for some reason." He grinned. "Besides, where would you take me that you could be seen with a Shareem?"

"I hadn't thought of that." She looked agitated. "I just wanted to go out, get away from here for a while." She glanced about the Spartan room. "Is this where Metri has put you? I apologize."

Rees followed her gaze, surprised. The room was plain, yes, but well-sealed and temperature-controlled and had every luxury. She should have seen what they made him live in at DNAmo.

"So it doesn't have pillows and piped music. Shareem don't need much."

She did not answer. She just stood there like she wanted to say something and didn't know how.

He didn't mind as long as he could look at her. She was beautiful, though she might not believe it.

She had a plumpness that was not fashionable, and she had curves. Who couldn't love those curves? But upper-class ladies liked to make themselves lean and flat and unattractive to men.

Whatever Rees didn't like about Lady Pet, she had at least let Talan be beautiful.

Talan had been even more beautiful that morning, when she'd laid down in the water and come and come. With her hair raining down her back to swirl in the stream, her eyes half closed, her face soft with ecstasy —

He got hard just thinking about it.

Correction, he'd had a hard-on as soon as she appeared in the doorway. He was perpetually hard around this woman.

"Rees," she said suddenly. "Take me somewhere."

He got up. He walked to her, drew her inside and let the door close. "We're somewhere now."

"No, I mean out of the house—somewhere I *can* be seen with a Shareem."

He traced her cheek. The scent of her danced in the air. "What's wrong, little Talan?"

She did not want to be placated. She stepped away from him. "I want to be with you, away from here. Take me—" She paused, cheeks flushing. "Take me to your world. To the back streets."

She said it like it was a distant planet. He smiled. "Sure you want to? It's not pretty and clean, like here."

She rubbed her arms, as though trying to scrape something off her sleeves. "I don't care. I just want out."

Out of her gilded cage? "Poor little rich girl," he teased. "All right. I'll take you. But if you want to keep your reputation, you'll have to go in disguise."

She looked intrigued. "I have a long cloak, and I can hide my face—"

He laughed. "No, baby. The minute anyone spots you in a rich cloak and veil, they'll peg you as high-born. You want to end up on a news digital?" He tugged off her veil, setting her hair free. "You need to hide in plain sight."

He gathered her hair in his hands, lifted it from her neck. "Pin that up in a knot. You have a short-sleeved tunic, maybe some pants to go under it? That would be perfect."

She grinned, getting into the spirit of it. "Lady Pet will kill me."

"Lady Pet probably put up her hair and went out on the town plenty. She looks the type."

"You might be right. I'll tell Metri to send the litter 'round."

He shook his head. "No litter, no bodyguards. Just you and me. We'll take the hovertrain."

Her eyes lit up. "I've always wanted to do that."

"Gods, you are a poor little rich girl. Go get ready. I'll wait for you downstairs."

They had to ditch Metri. The enclosed courtyard held another cool fountain and a place for getting in and out of a litter, and for some reason, Metri watched it anxiously.

Like two naughty servants, Talan and Rees hid in the shadows of the hall, waiting, but Metri wouldn't move.

Then Talan got the idea to send him a bogus call from upstairs, and when Metri, sighing, went to answer, she and Rees slipped through the courtyard and out into the road.

Talan flushed and grinned as Rees took her arm and started down the street in the direction of the station.

"Oh, gods, what if the neighbors see me?" she whispered, turning her face from the blank-walled houses.

"If they see us at all, they'll think we're two servants out to enjoy ourselves. And we are. Out to enjoy ourselves."

"I'm already enjoying it," she said shyly.

"You have a bad life if you think running down the street in the heat is fun."

"It is with you."

Don't look at me like that, sweet lady. You make me want to be a very bad Shareem.

They ran along, hand in hand, like a man and his girl off to catch a train.

The streets grew crowded as they neared the station. Shopping and restaurants for the rich were everywhere. The sudden sandstorm this morning had caught many by surprise. More than one restaurant was repairing broken awnings and fetching chairs smashed into neighboring restaurants.

At the same time, litters letting off well-born women, bodies covered against the sun, flanked the restaurants, and slim men in servants' garb bade the harried restaurant owners to let their ladies in for lunch.

Talan kept her head turned to Rees' shoulder as they hurried past and into the cool shade of the hover station.

Talan was ready to run across the platform and into the open doors of the nearest train, and Rees pulled her back, laughing. "You have to buy a ticket."

"What?"

He dragged her to a ticket dispenser. "A ticket. You can't ride for free."

She looked puzzled. "Can't I just fingerprint?"

"Yes, if you have an account. Do you?"

"I haven't the faintest idea."

"Then you buy a ticket." He pulled a credit strip out of the pocket of his air-cooled robe, the kind you bought in a corner store. He let the vending machine eat it for a minute, then it spit it out along with two plastic tokens.

He handed one to Talan who studied it like a woman might study a new diamond.

He took her by the arm and steered her to the two-tiered platform. She didn't want to give up her ticket. She wanted to save it, like a souvenir. He took it out of her reluctant hand and dropped it in the slot so the force shield would open and they could get on the train.

The trains were relatively empty in this part of town. They found a seat where they could sit side by side, and Rees slid his arm around her shoulders. She snuggled up to him.

He was surprised, he thought she'd be too cautious. But maybe she figured no one would know her in a hover-train. She was probably right.

The train pulled out into a cavern made by the backs of buildings. They glided along, the train held by so powerful a grav pull that even a sandstorm couldn't knock it loose.

Rees had sat through a storm in a train car once. The train had stopped, but though the car rocked and jolted, it never fell.

He remembered himself and all the other people in the car holding their seats, waiting for a boulder or something to come smashing through the transparent canopy, but nothing had happened.

The train went fairly slowly through the twisted corridors of the city. Rees had seen on digitals that in cities on a jungle world, they built long transparent tubes that snaked through the city and jungle, and the cars traveled through that.

He'd heard that on some other world, everyone, rich and poor, had their own little transport cars, which they put into free-fall tubes that would carry them to any part of the planet they wanted.

Talan peered out the window eagerly, but after a while, her eyelids drooped. You could only see so many back alleys and sand-filled lanes before you got tired of it.

She leaned her head on his shoulder. He kissed her hair.

It was hard to control himself when he was around her. He was stiffly erect, even now. Usually he could turn off his pheromone-tasting, woman-seeking cock, but not with her. He wanted her to bury himself in her and rock until he came.

He had never taken it this slow before. But he knew that as soon as he deflowered Talan, he would be finished. Talan would say goodbye, show him the door.

He didn't want that to happen too soon. He wanted to savor every minute of her.

But the longer he waited, the harder it would be to keep control. He wanted to make it good for her, but the part of him that he tried hardest to tame got hard just thinking about hearing her scream.

Damn, am I panting enough? Rio would laugh himself sick.

He woke her up when the train stopped at their destination. She blinked sleepy eyes at him, then smiled.

He helped her up and guided her off the train. Air whooshed as the doors closed behind them and the hover-train glided away.

"Where are we?"

She looked at the grimy station, the dispirited and half-working robots that swept trash and dust from the floor. One robot had broken down completely about six months ago, and still sat in the middle of the station.

"Pas City," Rees said. "The heart of the back streets, as you call them."

She glanced around dubiously as he led her out of the station.

Life was different here than in the rich part of town, People strode through the narrow and dirty streets shouting greetings to people they knew, shouting rude words at people in their way, shouting promises from storefronts that their prices were lowest.

Several black-haired women with surgically enhanced green eyes leaned over a rusted balcony above the street.

"Rees," one cooed. "Rees, sweetie, come and see me."

Talan glanced up at the woman and away, a flash of jealousy in her eyes.

Jealousy. That was a new one. Usually women liked for Rees to be jealous or at least to pretend to be.

Rees couldn't believe he'd thought that if she dressed like a lower-class girl, she'd fit in. She obviously had never walked alone on a street before. Talan tried to look at everything at once, actually listened to the vendors hawking their wares.

She stopped before a shop of cheap jewelry and gawked.

The man who ran the booth had lost several of his teeth and hadn't bothered to replace them. Maybe he thought the gap-toothed look would improve his sales. He smiled at Talan.

"What is this?" Talan touched a particularly glittery bauble hanging from a necklace.

"The lady has taste," the vendor said.

Rees tried not to roll his eyes. The man would have said that if she'd picked up a stray insect that had landed on the table.

"But what is it?" She lifted the necklace, mystified.

Rees took it from her. "It's a star dancer. Haven't you ever seen one?"

He opened the silver globe that hung from the chain. Holo-lights, red, blue, green, yellow, gold and silver, shot out of it and swirled together just above the two halves of the sphere. The lights danced and sparkled and twisted.

"Oh, how *beautiful*."

"Buy it for your lady," the vendor suggested. He would. "Two bits."

"Are you crazy?" Rees asked at once.

The vendor took on a look of cunning, anticipating talking Rees down to his real price. But Talan's eyes widened. "Two bits? That's so cheap. I'll take it."

The vendor goggled. Then he looked disappointed he hadn't asked for three.

"No, it isn't," Rees said. "It's robbery." He took his credit slip out of his pocket, made a face and handed it to the vendor. "But nothing's too good for my girl."

"No, Rees—" Talan stuck her hand out to take the credit slip back. Rees closed his hand on hers.

"*I said*, nothing's too good for my girl."

The vendor licked his lips greedily, stuck the slip into his handheld machine. He handed it back, two bits lighter, and Rees put it into his pocket. He took the necklace from Talan and clasped it around her neck.

"You're right, it's beautiful." He tilted her chin back, pressed a soft kiss to her lips.

She exhaled as he pulled away, her breath skimming his lips like a caress.

The vendor chuckled, breaking the moment. "I have plenty of pretty rings for a pretty lady. Cheap, too."

"Shut up, you old thief," Rees said. He put his arm around Talan's shoulders and guided her away.

The necklace bounced softly on Talan's chest as she followed Rees. She had to follow him, clinging to his hand, because the street was so crowded, they couldn't walk together.

People pushed and shoved and bumped right into her, sliding against her with their smelly bodies and rough clothes. It was all very strange.

Stranger was the look on Rees' face when he put the necklace around her neck. She'd seen naked hunger in his eyes. He hadn't even looked like that when he'd told her to sit down this morning so he could lick her.

Then he'd been smiling, teasing, half-triumphant.

She was so alone with him. She might be able to find her way back to the station, but she had no money with her. Talan never needed money. She always gave her fingerprint, and her account was charged.

Here she had no accounts, no credit slip, no friends, no acquaintances. Just Rees and the lifeline of his hand.

He could take her anywhere and do anything he wanted to her. She was at his mercy.

Maybe it was Rees, maybe it was the spell he cast, but she was not afraid. In fact, she liked it.

She watched him walking ahead of her, his broad shoulders swaying, his bare, brawny arm brushing back the folds of his cloak. He had strong hands. Strong fingers. She stroked her thumb softly along one of those fingers.

He turned his head, gave her a dark smile.

It was right then, she thought, that she *knew*.

Rees turned to an open doorway that looked like all the other doorways crowded on this street. Cloth strips that had once been red fluttered from the doorframe. They'd been fixed behind the storm door, so that the door could drop into place without impediment when a sandstorm blew up.

The door remained open this afternoon, and sand gritted under their feet.

More sand lay inside, like no one had bothered to sweep the floor after the storm. The room was bigger than Talan had thought, but mostly empty.

A couple of men sat on a bench on the other side of the room, huge mugs resting on their knees, their heads back against the wall. One snored.

A bar took up the entire back wall. Behind it, a tired-looking, but pretty young woman leaned on her elbows. The room was dim, and she blinked against the glare, trying to see who had come in.

A man came out of the shadows on the left side of the bar. He was tall and broad-shouldered like Rees. He wore a leather jacket that hung open to show a hard-muscled chest. His pants were leather, too, hugging his thighs and hips.

His black hair was caught loosely in a tail, and his face was square and handsome. He had deep-set blue eyes, a grin that was warm, and a voice that was big and booming.

"Rees!" He came across the room, clapped Rees hard on the shoulder. "About time you showed up."

Chapter Seven

ဆ

Talan stared at him. He was Shareem all right. He had the eyes, the build, the voice.

He went on jovially, "So what are you doing down here dressed like a rich boy?" His gaze swiveled to Talan, his eyes widened. "Oh, man. Who's the pretty?"

Rees drew Talan into the circle of his arm. "Her name is Talan. Talan, this is Rio. My sort-of friend."

"Your *only* friend, boy-o."

"He's a notorious liar. Don't trust him, don't believe him, don't listen to him."

Rio's grin widened. "I'm not as good a liar as you." He took Talan's hand. "Let me buy you a drink, sweetheart. I bet you're thirsty, walking around with him."

Rees' voice took an edge. "She's with me."

Rio cocked a brow at him. "That doesn't mean I can't be nice. You get tired of him, Talan, you find me and tell me where it hurts." He lowered one eyelid in a wink. "Or where you want it to hurt."

His Shareem touch sent a warmth through her, even though she tried to stop it. If he kept up, she'd be on her knees asking if she could unbutton his trousers.

Rees must have sensed this, because he firmly led Talan to the bar.

The young woman behind it gave him a smile of welcome. "Hey, Rees."

"Judith," Rees said warmly. "Get Talan a ginger mint." He named a drink high on flavor, low on alcohol.

"I can drink ale," Talan said quickly. Ale was what the lower-class servants drank. She'd never had it before, but this was an adventurous day.

Rees leaned to her, spoke into her ear. "Not with Rio here."

His voice tickled her senses, sent heat through her that far overshadowed Rio.

She glanced over at the black-haired man. He still watched her. He smiled, but there was something dangerous about him. She could feel it in the air, like a vibration surrounding him.

She sensed that the only reason Rio held back was because Rees stood between her and him. She suddenly felt glad she hadn't met the man without Rees present.

She looked at the woman called Judith. Judith had dark red hair pulled up in a sloppy bun, friendly brown eyes, and a pretty oval face. She dressed in a coverall, pants tucked into boots.

Talan leaned forward. "Excuse me, but do you have a — um, you know, a ladies?"

Judith grinned. "Sure. Let me show you."

She plunked two ales in front of Rees and Rio, and a tall glass of something minty-smelling in front of Talan. Then she dried her hands, motioned Talan to follow.

Judith took Talan to an alcove on the other end of the bar, pointed the way to the relieving room. "Don't let Rio scare you," she said softly. "He's got a kind heart, deep inside."

They both glanced back. Rio said something to Rees and laughed. Rees shook his head.

"Deep, deep inside," Judith finished with a grin. "The toilet's down there. It's clean."

It *was* clean, to give Judith credit. The facilities were up to date. Judith obviously took care of the place. She'd even scented the air.

Talan sterilized her hands, then took a moment to splash her face at the water basin. She needed to cool down. She was barely comfortable with one Shareem, and now she was confronted with two.

Rees' friend, Rio. The level *three*.

Judith might tell her not to be afraid, but she thought that fear was healthy about now.

You never knew what you really felt around Shareem, Talan was learning. Whenever she looked at Rees, she was struck with longing and hunger. Was that a natural response, or his Shareem tricks?

She wanted his hands on her, his mouth everywhere. She wanted him to lift her onto this wash basin and take her right here.

She suddenly imagined Rees spreading her, pushing his way in with his long, long cock.

Rio would walk in the room behind Rees, stand there watching. He'd look at her with his dark blue eyes, and smile that smile. She'd get more and more excited, beg Rees to take her harder and harder.

She'd look at Rio and he'd look at her, then Rees would groan and spill his seed deep inside her. Rio would wink at her and walk quietly out. It would be their secret.

She dragged in a breath, splashed more water on her face. What was wrong with her? She'd never thought of anything like that before, ever.

Rees was corrupting all her ideas. He'd come into her life—at her own stupid invitation—and was turning it inside out.

Meeting Rio wasn't helping.

Talan turned to the mirror and saw in dismay that her nipples were hard as little pebbles. They stood out through the thin dress.

She rubbed them. They just tingled and stood out even more.

Hurriedly she tried to think about ice cubes and the sandstorm that had torn the force field off the garden this morning.

Talan shivered. If Rees had not caught her, pulled her to safety, she could have died.

Her nipples went down a little, but she walked slowly out of the room, lingered in the alcove while she folded her arms over her chest and willed her body to *stop*!

Rio and Rees were talking. Their voices were low, but some trick of acoustics carried them to her. Judith was not at the bar, she served more ale to the older men in the corner, talking to them in her easygoing way.

Rio said, "You struck gold, my friend. Rich *and* hot." He stopped when Rees said nothing, frowned. "What's the matter?"

"Nothing. I just don't want to tell you the details. She asked me to teach her, so I'm teaching her." He sounded indifferent.

"The way she looks at you, you're doing a fine job." Rio took a sip of ale. "Want to do a double with her?"

Rees was quiet for a long moment. "No," he answered. "She's not ready."

"We could take turns then."

"She's not ready for that either."

Rio grinned. "What, is she a virgin?"

"As a matter of fact—"

Rio's eyes widened. "Swear to the gods?" His grin vanished. "Wait a minute, you mean she's *still* a virgin? After a night with you?"

"A night and a day," Rees said. "I'm taking it slow. She needs it slow."

"Sweet gods, why did a virgin who needs to go slow go out with *you*? She should have gone for a level one."

"She didn't know."

"So you're holding back? That must be hell."

Rees took a sip of ale. "It's not easy. She's—" But he did not finish.

Rio rested his hand on Rees' shoulder, looked reverent. "Man, you are braver than I thought."

Why? Talan wondered. *Why brave?* And why did Rio imply she'd made a mistake sending for Rees? Rees had been gentle—except when he'd been...not gentle. But he hadn't frightened her. Much. Not like Rio did.

"I commend you, my friend." Rio lifted his ale. "When she's ready for a double, you know where I'll be."

"Yes, horny."

Rio shrugged. "Hey, she's beautiful. I can't help myself. Judith, love..."

Judith went back to the bar with the empties, Talan backed into the shadows until she'd gone by. "What?"

"Ready to take us on again?" His voice had lowered to its seductive Shareem tone.

Judith snorted and slammed the glasses down. "The last time I went out with the pair of you, I was sore for weeks."

"I remember you enjoyed yourself, though."

Judith looked away, blushing. Rees laughed softly.

Talan stood in the shadows, trying to banish her dart of jealousy.

Why should she be jealous? She'd only known Rees a day. He'd been free to do what he liked, with whom he liked, before that.

She'd felt the same jealousy when that woman had leaned over the balcony on the street.

Maybe it was the way he was laughing now, in fond memory. Or maybe—

Maybe because it had just hit her what servicing Talan meant to him. Servicing. Nothing more.

She'd asked for a teacher, and he was teaching her. When he was done, he'd go back to the lady on the balcony or play a little with Judith. She should care less.

But pain burned through her, and her eyes stung with tears.

Well, she had a choice. She could get angry, tell Rees to take her home then send him away.

Or, she could put aside her petty jealousy and enjoy every single thing Rees had to teach her. He'd teach her until she'd learned enough.

And then she could consider herself a bold and daring woman. She'd found a Shareem, just like Lady Ursula in the diary, and thumbed her nose at philosophy.

Maybe later, she could come back down here, and find Rio…

As though he heard her thoughts, Rio turned and peered into the shadows of the alcove.

Talan gulped. She drew a breath, squared her shoulders, and walked briskly out, pretending she'd simply spent a long time washing her hands.

Rees turned. He smiled. He held out his hand, drew her into the circle of his arm. "Hey, baby, I missed you."

His eyes were warm, his smile fond. Her heart turned over.

He bent and kissed her. His lips were hot and hungry. She wound her arm around him, let him open her mouth with practiced, sweet kissing.

Rio snickered.

Rees broke the kiss. But he didn't look offended or embarrassed. He gave his friend an annoyed look and picked up his ale.

Talan drank her drink. It was slightly warm now, and very minty.

"Oh, Rees, I forgot." Judith reached under the bar, pulled out a plastic disk. "You got a message yesterday. They looked for you at home, then called here." She handed it to him.

Rees palmed the disk, studied it. "I'll take care of it." He looked at Rio, then back at the disk. "Judith," he said. "Don't let Rio eat her."

Judith smiled, shook her head.

Rees slid his hand down Talan's spine to rest on her backside. "Be right back, sweetheart."

He turned and sauntered to the alcove. Talan had seen the com-port there near the facilities. She was surprised he didn't have a handheld, but then she'd left her own handheld at home.

She already missed Rees' warmth. There was something about him, not just his enhanced body and the way she could make her hormones dance. His smile. She liked it, she wanted to see more of it.

Judith started washing glasses. With water. Bor Narga had plenty of water—deep wells drew it to the dry surface, which was why they could have gardens. That wasn't the problem. But no one washed things you drank from in water. They used a sterilizer.

Just one more clue that she did not belong here.

Rio moved to her so quietly she never heard him. She'd been watching Judith scrub glasses with a brush, and all of a sudden, she felt Rio's heat at her shoulder.

She turned her head. He caught her chin with his fingers.

Judith looked up, then gave them an "oh, it's harmless" look, and went back to work.

Rio stroked his thumb across Talan's lower lip. "So, what has Rees taught you about Shareem?"

His voice was low, silken, sultry. His good-natured grin was gone.

"Only a little," she stammered.

His thumb went back and forth on her lip. "What did he tell you about level three?"

She couldn't speak. Her throat was dry, like the sand on the floor.

"Bondage," Judith said flatly. "Everyone knows that, Rio."

Rio kept his eyes on Talan. Deep blue eyes, flecked with midnight black.

"It's not what you think it is," he said softly. "It's not confinement. It's surrendering and trusting, letting go. It's opening yourself. Putting yourself in the hands of another. Entirely."

His eyes grew darker, the irises widening.

Talan tried to turn her head, look to where Rees had gone, but she couldn't. Rio's gaze invited her to surrender to him. It promised that she would not regret it.

He lifted her hand in his large fingers. "I'd bind your wrists. Tight, but not so tight you wouldn't like it. Then I'd strip off your clothes one at a time. Or maybe rip them off, depending on how I felt." His hand closed, trapping her. "Then you'd kneel to me. And do whatever I wanted. *Absolute surrender.*"

Her heart hammered. She could feel herself getting wet, no matter how much she tried to stop it.

But she knew one thing. As gorgeous as Rio was, as mesmerized as he had her, she didn't want him.

She wanted Rees. She wanted Rees to touch her like this, Rees to say these things to her.

Rio went on. "You'd suck my cock, open your ass, whatever I wanted. You'd resist me. I'd punish you. By the end of the night, you'd be begging me to punish you. Loving it. You'd wrap my whip around you and rub your pussy on it, you'd love it so much."

He lifted her hand, flicked his tongue across her fingers. "How about it, Talan? We can let Rees watch, if you want."

Talan gulped. Her lips parted, and she wished the cream would stop.

No, she wished Rees would take her somewhere and lick it off her.

Maybe Rio was putting pictures in her head, but she had a sudden vision of herself, naked, her hands bound, kneeling in front of Rees, taking his cock in her mouth like he'd taught her. "That's it, Talan," he'd say hoarsely. "Suck me hard."

Rio would be there, watching with his dark eyes.

She gasped for breath. The vision fell away and it was just Rio, and the bar digging into her side, and Judith splashing water. "I think I'll stick with level two for now."

Rio looked puzzled. "Level two?"

"Rees is level two."

Rio and Judith exchanged a quick glance. Talan opened her mouth to ask a question, when the doorway darkened and two tall women came in from outside.

Rio looked at them, snarled a swear word, and backed away from Talan. The sexual miasma that Rio had wrapped 'round her vanished.

Judith did nothing. She didn't greet the women or offer to sell them drinks. She just went on washing glasses.

The two women wore gray overalls and a faint coating of sand. Both had ear- and mouth-pieces and carried handhelds. The first one grinned and walked over to Rio. "Okay, Shareem. Ident time."

Rio gave her a dark look. "This is getting boring. You idented me last week."

"I just seem to keep running into you. Come on."

Rio leaned against the bar. He was much taller than the woman, and that seemed to annoy her. "You know who I am, and you know where I am. I'm Rio and I'm standing right here. What do you need an ident for?"

The woman smiled at him, not a nice smile. "*I* know you're here, but the computer don't. So hurry up, Shareem, shove it in the slot. Isn't that what you're good at?"

Her partner snickered.

Rio jerked an ident card from his jacket, thrust it into the little machine she held out to him. "I wouldn't put anything in your slot, sweetheart. Not a damned thing."

The woman checked her handheld, kept smiling. "You would if I paid you."

"You will never have enough money, darling. Never, ever."

The woman got the insult, slammed her finger to the pad. "What's this? Looks like you're expired, Rio."

"*Cock.* I renewed the card last week. You know it."

"Hmm. The computer seems to think you haven't. If you come with me, we'll fix it. Might have to lock you up a while, though, until the process is through. Can't have a Shareem with no ident wandering around loose."

"Lick me." Rio was furious. But Talan knew the woman could do it. Shareem weren't people. Not real people.

"Leave him alone," Talan said suddenly. "I will vouch for him."

The words did not have their intended effect. The woman should have recognized a high-born, bowed her head, looked sheepish, and given Rio back his ident. Maybe even apologize.

Instead, she looked Talan up and down and barked a laugh. "Who the hell are you?"

Talan lost her temper. "I am Lady Talan d'Urvey, and don't you *dare* address me in that manner."

She'd learned something living with Lady Petronella all these years. Her voice rang with crisp authority.

The two women stared at her. So did Rio and Judith. Even the old men in the corner woke up and listened.

The first woman gave her an insolent look. "Oh, yeah? Where's *your* ident?"

"I do not have one. I am not required to carry one to submit to the likes of you."

"Is that so?"

Talan held up her finger. "Do you have a fingerprint machine? You do know that all officers of the law are required to carry one? That is, if that *is* what you are."

They weren't. She didn't know quite who these women were, but they were not police, people who kept order and were respected.

Whatever they were, they'd been given a low job, and they struck back at Rio because they could.

The woman, with bad grace, removed a slim handheld from her coverall, held it out to Talan, still smirking. Talan did not want to touch the pad because it was greasy, but she pressed her finger quickly to it. She reached for a cloth on the bar and studiously wiped her finger.

The first woman stared at the handheld in some dismay. The second asked, "What?"

"She really is Lady Talan d'Urvey." The woman looked up, swallowed. Her pallor enhanced the dirt on her face. "Sorry, my lady. I didn't know."

"Give him back his ident card," Talan said sharply.

The woman removed Rio's card from the slot, handed it to him. He took it without snatching and tucked it back into his coat.

"Go," Talan finished. "If you harass this man again, I will hear of it, and it will not go well for you."

The first woman looked cowed, but the second drew up her courage. "My lady. Shareem ain't men."

Talan bathed her in a freezing stare that would make Lady Petronella proud. "They look like men. They talk like men. They seem to be men."

"They ain't," said the woman, defiant. "They're *rutters*."

An awful silence fell. The woman grew red, tried to look anywhere but at Talan.

"When you speak to me, you will answer my questions and not offer opinions," Talan said coldly. "Now go."

The first one said, "Yes, my lady." She turned around and nearly ran out of the bar. The second scuttled out after her.

Rio let out a whoop of laughter. Judith applauded. Rees came out of the back just then.

Talan wondered why he'd deliberately stayed out of the way. He'd behaved as though he hadn't wanted the women to see him at all.

But he'd clearly heard everything. He smiled and slid his arm around Talan's waist. "That's my girl."

She felt cozy against the warmth of his body. "But why were they identing you?" she asked Rio. "She knew who you were. What was the point?"

"The point," Rees explained, "is that they're making sure we Shareem stay where we're supposed to, like good little boys."

"I don't understand."

"We're not allowed to leave the planet," Rio said.

"Why not?"

"Because we Shareem might do something bad, like settle down," Rio said. "Get married. Have a life."

"What is wrong with that?" Talan asked, puzzled.

"They don't want Shareem having kids," Rees said. "Reproducing our enhanced genes the old-fashioned way. If we stay in the city, get our inoculations, then we're allowed to live."

"But that's not right."

"Ain't she sweet?" Rio asked no one in particular.

"It was the bargain when DNAmo let the Shareem go," Rees said. "It was either that or get hunted down."

"Some got hunted down, anyway," Rio said, anger on his face. "It wasn't pretty."

"So you agreed?" Talan asked.

"I wouldn't say *agreed*," Rees said.

"One day, though, I'm blasting off this rock," Rio put in. "Going somewhere that gorgeous guys like me are appreciated."

Judith had gone back to washing glasses. "You say that all the time, Rio."

"Yeah, but one day."

He and Rees exchanged a glance that Talan couldn't interpret. Rees gave his friend the barest nod.

Then Rees slid his arm around Talan's waist. "Time to go, babe."

He led her to the door. Judith looked up, smiled. "Don't be a stranger, Talan."

Rio found his grin again. "Hey, Rees. You need help explaining anything to her, you just give me a call."

"Right," Rees said. He went through the door first, checked the street, then reached back for Talan. "Stay out of trouble, Rio."

"Hey, I *am* trouble," Rio chuckled, and then Rees led Talan away.

Chapter Eight

ဆ

The streets, if anything, had gotten more crowded. Rees held Talan's hand tightly, afraid that if she slipped away, he'd never find her again.

She might be Lady Talan d'Urvey, and she might have scared the patrollers, but she'd never last by herself in these streets.

Rees had no business bringing her down here. He knew that, now.

Rio had nearly swayed her. Rees had smelled it when he'd returned, the tang of her female juices that had been worked up. Rio had worked her up. She'd looked guilty.

A pain had jabbed his heart, catching Rees by surprise.

Rees couldn't believe it. He was jealous. Of Rio.

No, maybe he was just worried for Talan. She was so innocent. Even if she'd read books and taken classes about sex, she didn't know how dangerous desire was.

Rio was up front about how bad he was and what a woman could expect from him. Rees hid it inside him. Ladies thought Rees was gentle, until it was too late. So who would Talan be better off with?

Rees also had things to take care of. The message Judith had given him was from another off-world pilot he'd been in contact with. The pilot had decided he wanted nothing to do with Rees and Rio. Too hot for him. Unless Rio wanted to pay him a fortune.

Rees had argued but had to give up. He had other connections, but it was going to take time. Rio was too impatient. He might screw everything up just by doing something impetuous or opening his big mouth.

But Rio was the only person on Bor Narga who knew the secret of Rees. Rio had kept the secret, Rio had been his friend. Rees owed him.

Rees owed Talan, too. She looked at him and smiled her sweet smile and did things to his insides.

He wanted Talan in every way possible. But he also wanted to protect her. It was weird.

Her hand was soft and trusting in his. Just that light touch fired up his hormones.

He dragged Talan out of the crowd to a relatively calm spot near some buildings. He pulled her into his arms and kissed her.

Her sweet lips responded to his instantly. Innocent kisses that trusted him.

He so wished he could trust himself.

"We should go back," he said.

Talan looked up at him, her eyes shining. "I don't want to. Not yet."

"You don't belong here."

He tried to sound severe. He would like nothing better than to wander around hand in hand with Talan all afternoon. Like sweethearts.

"What did Rio say to you?" he asked.

She turned bright red. "Oh, he — well —"

He put his fingers under her chin. "Tell me."

She looked around quickly, but the people passing by on the street weren't listening or even looking at a Shareem and his girl.

She wet her lips. "He said he wanted to use his whip, and I'd be begging for it."

She was embarrassed. Actually embarrassed. Most women Rio charmed were drooling on themselves by the time he finished.

"And what did you say?" Rees asked.

"What on earth could I say? No one has ever said things like that to me before."

"Did you agree to meet him later?"

She looked bewildered. "No. Why should I?"

That strange jealousy bugged him again. "Well, don't. No matter how pretty he talks, I don't want you anywhere near him. Not without me."

He turned abruptly and started to lead her away.

"*I* sent for *you*," she said behind him.

He stopped. A man in a faded robe ducked around them with a snarl.

"What are you talking about?"

"Lady Pet brought you home for me. To teach me."

"Yeah, so?"

Her eyes were sparkling, her chin lifted. "So I can always ask Rio, too."

He wondered how hard it had been for her to say that. The timid lady was learning independence.

Rees growled. He grabbed her hand in a hard grip, dragged her back into the crowd.

"Where are we going?" she panted.

"Home."

"But I said I didn't want—"

Her words were cut off as they zigzagged through the crowd.

Rees had no intention of taking her back to Lady Petronella's. Not after she'd said that.

She was going to learn just who was in command here.

Rees led her a few streets over, through a bazaar and down a quieter side street. Here the houses were neater, the street washed clean of the sand of today's storm. A few hover vehicles were parked against the sides of the tall houses.

A man in gaudy robes came out of one of the houses. He had blond hair and blue eyes and opened one of the hover cars. "Hey, Rees," he said.

Rees said "hey" back. The man ogled Talan, but Talan didn't notice. She was too busy looking around.

Rees palm-keyed open the door of a house halfway along the street.

The elegant tiled hall, cool and dark after the heat of the sun, soothed Rees' feet even through his shoes.

On the left side of the hall lay a drop tube. Without explaining, Rees led Talan to it and stepped inside.

The null-grav unit kicked in, and they floated gently down to the floor below.

He led Talan out of the tube and into another elegant hall. She waved her hand in front of her face.

"Those always make me queasy."

Rees almost smiled. But he wasn't here for laughs.

He palm-keyed the single door on the bottom floor. It opened readily, and he took Talan inside.

"Where are we?" she breathed.

"I told you," he said, shutting the door and sliding his hands around her waist from behind. "Home."

She looked around eagerly. "Oh. *Your* home."

Home was an apartment that was comfortable, if not showy. Rees liked things simple, clean.

"Why did you bring me here?" she asked.

He leaned down, nibbled the shell of her ear. "To spank you. I didn't want to do it on the street."

She looked back at him, eyes wide. "You don't really mean—?"

"Yes, I do."

He lifted her, carried her to the nearest chair, sat down and tumbled her across his knee. He grabbed the skirts of her robes, hiked them to bare her pretty ass, and started spanking.

* * * * *

Back at the bar, Rio moodily watched Judith. She finished her washing, then retrieved the glasses the two old men had left on the table.

Rio was pissed at the patrollers, but he had to laugh at the way Talan had sent them running.

What a sweet, pretty girl. Damn, he'd wanted to fill her. She got him all hard and ready. He'd hoped that Rees would invite him along when they went.

He could have plugged her from behind while she rode Rees. Or Rees could have licked her pussy while Rio was in her backside. Either way, she'd have been screaming.

He drank his ale and wiped condensation from his fingers. A pretty pussy she'd have, too.

But Rees hadn't asked. Rio thought about the way Rees had said, "She's with me." Like she was special to him.

He started to chuckle. *You'd better watch it, boy-o. That girl will break your heart.* She'd tear it to bits before Rees even knew it.

"You staying or going, Rio?"

Judith took the glasses behind the bar, looked at Rio.

"What did you think of her?" he asked Judith.

"Who? Rees' girl?" She shrugged. "Cute. But with claws. Only, she hasn't figured out she has the claws yet. But she will."

"Yeah, she'd have been good in a threesome." He took another gulp of ale. "*Damn* good."

"That's all you think about, you know."

He laughed. "You were thinking about it too, babe. I saw you looking at Rees. You were wishing he'd ask to make it a foursome."

Judith blushed. "Okay, maybe."

"So how about it? Do a foursome? Just you and me?"

"Uh, Rio, that would be a twosome."

Rio shrugged. "So we'll be creative. Come on, Judith. I'm screaming horniness over here, and so are you. I can taste it."

Judith opened her mouth to argue, then she shook her head. "Let me close up."

Rio watched her come around the bar again and tap the controls on the walls. The storm door slid down, and the lights dimmed.

"You have a nice ass," he told her.

"Thank you. So do you."

He met her in the middle of the floor.

Leather creaked as he yanked open the front of her coveralls and thrust his hands inside. She was bare underneath, like he'd thought. Too hot to be anything else.

He pulled her body against his and kissed her, hard. She grabbed his arms, fingers sinking into the black leather. He licked her from lips all the way down her throat. She leaned her head back, her bare breasts thrusting against his chest.

He lifted her up, letting her body rub his groin.

"Not here," she gasped. "Upstairs."

He turned and carried her to the door that led to her apartment. She thumbed open the lock, and he started to climb the narrow, cool stairs.

He made it halfway. Rio kissed her again, then laid her facedown on the stairs.

He yanked her coverall from her body. There she was, bare-assed, trying to steady herself on the stairs, trying to crawl upward.

He was too throbbing and crazy with heat to let her. He had to do it now.

He jerked his leggings down, letting his arousal tumble free. Judith looked back at it in panic. Shareem were bigger than normal men, and Rio was damn big, even for a Shareem.

"Oh gods, Rio."

"Too late to pray, babe."

He opened her legs and slid himself right into her cunt. She screamed. He pumped.

He thought about Rees pumping himself into pretty Talan. Rees would be hard and excited, his face drawn in concentration. Talan would be squirming, pleading, begging, wet and tight.

Oh, man, Rees must be having a good time.

Rio braced himself on the stairs above Judith, surrounding her with himself.

Her wet tunnel squeezed him again and again. She screamed and writhed, coming already, her body rubbing against the stairs.

Rio took hold of her hair, wrapped it around his hand. He rode her, hips crashing into her backside. She screamed until her voice went raw.

He came pretty fast because Talan had gotten him so hard. The girl had looked startled when he'd told her she'd wrap his whip around her body and make love to it, but the idea hadn't scared her.

She'd wanted it.

Better watch it, Rees, he thought. Poor guy.

He slammed his full length into Judith, and spilled his seed. Judith moaned and whimpered.

He let go of Judith's hair, and she collapsed onto the stairs, sliding off his hard cock, which was slick with her juices and his come.

Rio sat down on the stairs, panting, running his hands through his sweat-soaked hair. Judith turned over and gave him a rueful smile. "Damn, Rio."

"I can't help it. I love your pussy."

She laughed breathlessly. She pulled herself up, lifted her coveralls over her legs, but didn't fasten them again.

She moved down a few steps, then sank to her knees and put her mouth over his still hard cock.

"Baby," he murmured. He threaded his hands through her loosened hair. "You know just how to do it."

"You taught me," she said.

He laughed, then groaned as her practiced mouth went all over his cock. He liked Judith, they were friends. He liked being with a woman just because she wanted to be with him.

He'd stay all night if she wanted. He had his accoutrements with him. He never went far without him. He had his whip coiled and ready in an inner pocket of his jacket. Judith probably had some cream down in the bar. And let's see, what else?

He removed the thin manacles from inside his jacket and clicked one around Judith's wrist. She stared at him, mouth open.

"Ask me to stay, baby," he said. "We'll have some fun."

She looked at him, her lips all wet from his cock. She considered. His rod started throbbing again as her pheromones scented the stairwell.

She grinned suddenly, eyes warm. "I'm going to regret this, I know it."

Rio grinned back. It was going to be a good night.

Chapter Nine

ஐ

Talan's rear hurt and stung. She'd never felt anything like it.

She still hung upside down over Rees' lap, her hair in her face. His hand rested on her ass, cool on her burning skin.

"No one has ever dared spank me before," she gasped.

"No?"

"No."

He gave her one more slap. She yelped. He righted her, planted her on his lap and grinned into her face.

"That's because you've never been bad."

"Why do you keep saying I'm bad?"

"Because you are. Telling me you're going to run off to Rio. I should have spanked you harder."

"Oh." He was playing a game. That's what a level two Shareem did, played games.

She could play, too. She looked at him from under her lashes. "Maybe I *will* run off with him."

Something went dark in his eyes, and then he smiled again. "Uh-oh, you just said the wrong thing."

He flipped her over. He was so strong, he did it before she could stop him. "No, Rees!" she laughed and screamed at the same time.

Smack, smack, smack. Her butt was going to be raw.

It hurt, and at the same time it didn't. It stung, and it was fun. How strange was that?

Rees rubbed his hand across her ass. "How does that feel?"

"Ouch."

He laughed. He pulled her skirts down and set her on her feet. "Are you going to say bad things to me again?"

She put her finger to her mouth, considered. "Maybe."

"You're so adorable when you do that."

Adorable. That wasn't dignified.

He just sat there and smiled. Her heart turned over.

This was wrong. She shouldn't be here. She should be at home, studying her books, memorizing pithy sayings of philosophers. She should not be playing games with a level two Shareem in his own house. She should not be warming every time he smiled.

His face was square and handsome, his eyes so blue. When he smiled she wanted him to take her into his arms and kiss her, just like he had on the street.

Wouldn't it be nice if he really wanted her? If he wasn't just pretending?

To cover her confused thoughts, she walked away from him. The room was small.

He had a monitor in one corner and a couple of disks in front of it. He also had a picture disk with a photo of himself, Rio, and Judith in it. Rio had his arm around Judith's neck, and all three were laughing.

Talan turned around. "Rees."

The way he looked at her made her heart beat fast. His Shareem-blue eyes warmed her from across the room.

"Rees, I think I'm ready."

"For what, bad girl, more spanking?"

"No." She twisted her fingers together. "For—penetration."

His smile vanished. "Call it by its right name, Talan."

She thought of what she'd said to him in the garden, and later in the bathroom. She took a deep breath. "For fucking." She came closer to him. "I want you to fuck me."

He sat so still. A muscle moved in his face, and that was all.

She walked to him, put her hands in his broad ones.

"Please fuck me, Rees."

His lashes came down to shield his eyes. "You aren't ready."

"I am." She began to feel desperate. "I *am* ready, Rees. You showed me how to feel good and how to give you pleasure. Now I want the rest of it. I want you inside me."

He looked up at her. His eyes were bluer than ever, the irises filling the white. "You're not ready for me. If I was a normal man, maybe, but I'm—"

"Shareem," she finished. "I know."

She waited for him to smile, to touch her face, but he just looked at her. "My cock is big."

"I know." She remembered the taste of it in her mouth. "I like it."

He gave her the ghost of a grin. "It's huge. And your pussy's small. It'll hurt you."

She wasn't so sure. "It's pretty wet already," she said softly. "Maybe if we go slow."

Rees closed his hands on hers in a crushing grip. "With you, Talan, I won't be able to go slow."

She got excited and scared at the same time. "You know—" she gave him a sly look, "—I can always go back and ask Rio."

That got him.

Rees' grip went tighter. "The *hell* you will."

Her excitement mounted. She knew he was increasing her excitement with his voice and his touch, and she didn't care.

"Maybe I don't want to stay with you anymore. Maybe I want to go with him."

He jerked her close. He breathed hard, his eyes getting darker. "Maybe you need another spanking."

She liked this game. She felt her mind go slightly mushy as he used his Shareem technique. "Make me stay with you," she breathed.

He pinched her jaw between his thumb and fingers. "Don't, Talan. I'm not playing."

Of course he was. That's what level twos did. She touched his face. "Make me yours."

His skin was hot. His grip tightened. It hurt. "Don't. Tempt. Me," he growled.

She smiled.

"Oh gods," he said.

He let go of her and stood up. He was so tall. His shoulders were broad, his arms corded with muscle.

Something inside her said she should be very afraid of him. But her mind spun with whatever he did to her, and she could only smile hotly.

"Don't resist me," he said.

She shook her head. Her loosened hair slid over her shoulders. It felt sensual.

"Did you bring a change of clothes?" he asked.

She gave him a puzzled look. "Of course not—"

"Too bad." He grabbed the neck of her tunic and ripped it open to her waist.

She gasped as the artificially cooled air touched her skin. Her breasts were standing firm and round, her nipples pointing right at him.

"Beautiful," he whispered. "I knew you'd be beautiful."

"You're beautiful, too," she murmured in response.

He was. He was the most beautiful man she'd ever seen.

"Don't try to get on my good side," he said with a warning look.

Playing was fun, even if a little scary. Lady Ursula had written all about playing with her Shareem.

"Spank me again," she begged.

"I'll spank you when I'm good and ready."

He grabbed her and crushed a kiss to her lips.

It was not so much a kiss as ravishing her mouth. She couldn't breathe. She clutched his arms. He was *strong*.

He pulled his mouth from her. "Get on the bed."

His bed was a bunk built into the wall. It was surrounded on three sides and had soft lights above that came on when she scrambled up onto it.

The bed was wide and long, but he was a large man, after all.

She faced him on her knees, her tunic ripped, her breath coming hard. He pulled off his robe, and then his tunic.

She was right, he was beautiful. His chest was hard with muscle, dusted with curls of gold. His stomach was flat, muscles taut past his navel to the thong that rode low on his hips.

She remembered watching him in the holo-block that day, weeks ago, remembered the sun on his bronzed backside, the shadows in the dents above his butt.

"You were the best Shareem they made, weren't you?" she whispered. "The most beautiful and the best."

His eyes went all blue again. She reached for him.

He shoved her hands away. "Lay down."

Whatever he was doing to her mind, he was good at it. She plopped onto her back.

He came closer. He smelled like dust and the tang of sweat.

"I'll give you a chance to run," he said, his voice low.

Talan thought about it. Her body didn't want to get up and leave. She shook all over, every nerve humming.

"Let me stay." She tried to smile. "Whatever you are doing to my mind won't let me leave anyway."

"I'm not doing anything to your mind, baby. You're doing it all yourself."

Talan didn't believe him. Whatever he wanted her to do, she would do. She couldn't help it.

"I wish you'd run," Rees said. "Then I could chase you."

A dark flutter stirred in her stomach. "You've already caught me."

He gave her an odd look and didn't answer. He leaned over her, put his hands on either side of her head.

His tail of blond hair fell over his shoulder and brushed her face. She caught it in her mouth.

"Hey," he said.

She smiled at him around it.

He twitched the tail out of her mouth. "You're not doing what you're supposed to do."

"I don't know what I'm supposed to do."

His eyes were midnight blue, now, black flecks swirling in them. "You are supposed to be afraid of me."

She touched his lips, satin-smooth. "Why?"

"Because I'm Rees."

What was that supposed to mean?

"I like you being Rees."

He looked at her like he didn't quite believe her. There was something behind his eyes she didn't understand.

His skin was scorching hot and he breathed hard, his cock was swelling and rising.

"I told you not to try to get on my good side," he said.

"Are you trying to frighten me, Shareem?" She twined her arms around his neck. "Is that the game we're playing this time?"

He came closer, nipped her lips. "Are you sure it's just a game?"

He kissed her. It wasn't as harsh as the last kiss, but slow and deep and possessive.

"Are you sure?" he asked again.

Her cunt was all wet and wanted him bad. "I'm sure I'm with you," she whispered. "And that's exactly where I want to be."

He looked down at her for a long time. His arms were taut, taking the strain of his weight.

"Talan. You are so going to pay for being so cute and sweet."

She wasn't sure what he meant, but anything he said now was drilling excitement through her.

"Are we going to fuck?" she said, voice shaking. "Or not?"

"Oh, you are *so* going to pay."

"When?" she asked.

"Right now, baby. Spread your legs."

She spread her thighs, already anticipating his touch. He'd driven her wild this morning with his tongue.

But he was right. It would hurt, and she should be afraid.

She put her hand down to her pussy, all wet and creamy. "Make me not care if it hurts," she said. "You can do that, can't you? With your Shareem — whatever it is?"

He nodded once. "I can. Or you can run to your clinic and not feel anything."

The clinic seemed cold and far away and foolish.

"No. I want you."

"I know you want me." He drew his fingers along her cunt. "Your pussy is so slick."

"Will you go in, now? Please?"

Her opening was wide, begging for him.

"I told you, I'll fuck you when I'm good and ready."

"Please, Rees, do it now."

He got off the bed.

She lay there, stunned and suddenly cold. She reached for him. "Rees, don't go."

"I'm not going anywhere, babe."

He opened a cupboard, pulled out a tube of something. He also took down a sun blanket.

Rolled up, it made a hard, firm pillow.

He brought it to her. "This goes under your hips."

Deftly, he slid his arm around her back, raised her, and slid the rolled-up blanket beneath her.

She felt funny, her back bent, her hips lifted to him.

He took off the thong. His cock was huge, long and hard, pushing out from the dark blond curls at its base.

He trickled something from the tube onto his finger, and brushed it onto his cock.

"Spread it on me," he commanded, tossing the tube aside.

Talan reached up. The lubricant was cool, but not cold, slick and wet.

His cock was so big. She spread the lube all over it while he knelt above her.

"That's it, sweetheart. This will make it go in easier."

His fists were clenched, the sinews standing out in his arms.

She liked touching his cock. It felt so nice under her fingers, smooth and soft, at the same time it was hard. The harder it was, the more she liked it.

She wanted to take it in her mouth and suck and suck, like he'd taught her this morning.

She wanted to run her tongue around the tip.

She wanted to bite it, just hard enough to make him say ouch.

She wanted it in her, all the way to his balls.

"Now, Rees?" she asked.

"Now, baby."

She released her hold. Her whole body shook. The rolled-up blanket was cool beneath her backside.

He put his hands on her knees, pushed them apart. He leaned over her, taking his weight on his hands, and put that huge cock right against her opening.

She gasped. The tip nudged its way in.

He was slick and there was no friction to stop him. He would slide all the way in, and it would hurt.

"Rees," she said, panicked. She clutched his forearms.

"It's all right, baby," he said, his voice Shareem soothing. "I'll make it good."

"It will hurt. You said it would hurt."

He put his face close to hers. "I was lying, baby. Just playing."

"Were you?" she asked hopefully.

"Look at my eyes," he said softly. "And feel me."

She looked. His eyes were blue, deep and large and drawing her in. She felt her panic ease, her limbs stop shaking.

His body was warm along the length of hers, his breath on her face hot. His hair brushed her shoulder.

Her mind relaxed. She could only think of the blue of his eyes, his warmth, and being surrounded by him.

"There," he said. "Here we go."

In one long move, he slid himself in.

* * * * *

One of the DNA programmers who'd volunteered to turn herself loose in a holo-simulation with R294E8S swore he had empathic abilities. The woman had to have counseling therapy for months after the experiment.

Another of the female scientists had helped him get free. She'd been found in nothing but her lab coat, huddled by the door of his room in a daze.

She'd had to have counseling, too.

Rees didn't know what all he could do, either. He only knew that to survive he had to lay low and pretend to be an everyday, average Shareem.

Rees knew that he could calm a woman simply by wanting her to be calm. He didn't have to touch her, he only had to look at her.

He could make a woman his slave.

He'd done it before, and they'd wept when he'd finished and left them.

Under him, he felt Talan grow warm and limp and receptive. He pushed himself further in.

She was hot and tight. He threw back his head in unbelievable ecstasy. The barrier within her moved, and broke.

He saw pain flood Talan's eyes. He smothered it with excitement.

She moaned and lifted her hips. *That's right, baby. Let me.*

She was sweet. She smelled good.

He went in farther. Her pussy pulsed around him. He'd never felt anything so good in his life.

He'd meant to just rest inside her, let her get used to the feel. But he wanted more and more and more.

His hips rocked. Her face twisted in passion. The hurt had gone and he knew she was feeling good.

You belong to me, he made her believe. *You're mine, and you'll beg me to do to you whatever I want.*

"Rees," she moaned. "*Please.*"

"Please what, darling?" he said. "Please what?"

"Fuck me."

"I am, beautiful."

He moved himself in and out. The friction was hot and good.

"Rees, gods. What do I feel?"

"What I want you to feel," he whispered.

"You're so big. I can't—"

"Yes, you can." He kissed her lips. "You're taking it, Talan. Every inch of it. You love it."

"I do love it."

"I love feeling you too, sweetheart."

He stroked her, in and out and in again. Her cunt was swallowing him. It was wet and slick and squeezing him hard.

Gods, he wanted her forever. Not just now, not just to teach her, but for always.

The thought was so strong, it almost pulled him out of his ecstasy.

Not quite. He kept going, kept riding her. She squirmed and squealed, loving what he did.

"It's good," he murmured. "This is good fucking, Talan."

She made another wordless noise, lost in joy.

He kissed her again. She tasted good. He licked her skin.

He smelled her sex on the air, smelled the sweet scent of her hair. He kissed her forehead and plowed her some more.

Would her ass be as good? he wondered. He wanted her ass, he wanted her in every way, and he'd make her beg him for it.

He sensed danger, but he couldn't stop to worry about it. She wanted him to show her what sex was. Well, he would show her every single thing about it. Every single way to fuck.

"Beg me for more, Talan."

Her eyes squeezed shut. "More, Rees, please."

He slid even further in, buried all the way to his balls. She whimpered.

"Do you love it, Talan?"

"Yes," she breathed. "I love it. I love you."

"I know, baby. I'm making you say it."

She opened her eyes. The blue of them held anguish. "No, I mean—"

"Oh, gods, no. What the hell—?"

He was coming. A black tide of excitement swept over him.

Rees had wanted to go for another hour or so. But he was coming, now. Her sweet tight cunt was making him come.

"Rees." She had tears on her face. He licked them off.

"Talan, baby, take my come."

He shot it deep into her, hot and thick.

She came too. He laid down on her as she squirmed and screamed and raked her nails down his back.

He gave her one more thrust, filling her to the brim, then he let out his breath.

Her hips thrust against his, hard, four or five more times, riding it out until the very end.

Then she collapsed.

Everything quieted.

Talan opened her eyes, smiled at him dreamily.

He raked her hair from her face. He was shaking and sweating. He'd just come and come and come, and her sweet little pussy was already making him hard again.

"You're beautiful," he whispered.

He kissed her swollen lips.

"I liked that," she said. She brushed her palm over his shoulder. "It was much better than I thought it would be."

He stared. "You've just been screwed by a Shareem and that's all you can say?"

"I said it was *much* better."

He chuckled. His engorged cock gave a throb. "Want to go again?"

She looked hopeful. "Can we?"

"All night, if you want it."

"Yes. I want it."

"Then ask me." He nipped her lips. "No, beg me."

"Fuck me all night, Rees," she said.

"Say please, little girl."

"Please, Rees. Please fuck me all night, pretty please."

His cock danced inside her. "And this from the woman who was going to give herself to philosophy."

"I will. Later. First, fuck me. Fuck me all night, Rees."

He did.

All through the afternoon and well into the dark hours, Rees drove his needy cock into her.

He showed her how to straddle him, pleasuring herself. He showed her how to lay with her ass on the edge of the bed while he lifted her legs and penetrated her. He liked it best when he lay on top of her, where he could hold her and kiss her.

By the time she fell asleep, he'd fucked his lady five times, and still his cock begged for more.

Chapter Ten

ஒ

Talan woke later that night to find herself snuggled naked against Rees.

His arm lay across her abdomen and his breath, sonorous and slow, warmed her ear.

She thought about everything they'd done and blushed. She thought about it again, and smiled.

Having her very own Shareem was educational.

And fun.

Lady Ursula had written about this in her diary. She'd had a level one Shareem, and her descriptions of his warm, slow hands on her body had fired Talan's imagination.

Rees was a level two, so it must be different. Rees was wild and laughing and teasing.

He was sound asleep now. Sleep relaxed his muscles, and with his Shareem eyes closed, he looked like a normal man.

A gorgeous, normal man who'd made love to her all night.

She was curious about his life before she'd met him. She wanted to know all about him. Soon, she'd have to let him go.

Soon, all she'd have would be her diary account, something to read and remind herself what he'd been like.

Talan gently eased out from under his arm. He frowned in his sleep, but didn't wake.

She stood beside the bed and looked down at him for a long time, then she leaned over and pressed a kiss to his forehead.

That didn't wake him up either. His skin had cooled, no longer burning hot like when he'd made love to her.

She'd have to ask him about that. She'd been hot and flushed, too, but nothing like he'd been. A normal man would have been burning up with fever at that temperature.

The high window above the bed showed black darkness. Talan walked to the bathroom, feeling a bit sore. The soreness didn't make her want to wince. It made her want to giggle.

The bathroom was clean and neat, except for a tunic he'd dropped in a corner. She picked it up the tunic and smoothed it out. The fabric was thick and sun-protective, and expensive. She folded it and left it on a shelf.

She used the necessary, then sterilized her hands and face.

She noticed he had a water shower, not a body sterilizer. She was tempted to use it, but she decided to first send a message to Lady Petronella.

Talan left the bathroom and quietly crossed the room to Rees' monitor. She sat gingerly on a chair in front of the terminal, and input a text message to Lady Pet telling her she was in the city with Rees and not to worry.

Once the message was gone, she remained in the chair, studying the picture of Rees, Rio, and Judith next to the terminal. All three were laughing. She felt a pang of envy.

Judith wasn't a rich woman looking for a night of forbidden pleasure with a Shareem. She talked to Rio and went out with him because she liked him, and he liked her. Talan envied their easy comradeship. She and Rees were pretending to have such a relationship right now, but Talan knew that would soon end.

She touched a button to scroll through the picture monitor. There were more pictures of Rio and some of Rees or Judith with him. One was on a tropical beach—a holo-room.

Rio was naked except for a loincloth, and he had a very nice body, indeed. Talan felt a bit disloyal to Rees for looking at it, but she could not help herself. Her womanly instincts made her stare.

Rio was posing and being silly. Rees stood next to him wearing a sleeveless tunic and rolling his eyes at Rio's antics.

Talan smiled and scrolled past the picture.

She noticed that in all the pictures, while Rio and Judith hung on each other and laughed, Rees stood a little apart from them, like he didn't quite belong. She'd sensed that in the bar, too. She wondered why that should be. Maybe Rees was different because he was more thoughtful. He had brains. So did Rio, she sensed, but Rio liked his bad-boy act.

She scrolled to the next picture. This one was of Rio with a different woman. The woman had brown hair and a pretty face. She wore upper-class robes, and Rio had his arm around her.

The next four pictures were of her and Rio, too, in various places around the city.

Another upper-class woman taken with a Shareem. Talan didn't recognize the woman, which was odd. The woman was not from off-planet—her robes and features were definitely Bor Nargan.

A pair of strong arms slid around her waist, and Rees leaned down and kissed her neck.

She felt herself melt to him again, felt her mind succumb to his Shareem presence.

"Who is she?" she asked, touching the screen.

Rees looked. "Her name was Serena."

"She likes Shareem."

"She liked Rio. And he liked her. A lot."

Talan looked up at him. "What happened?"

"Nothing. Serena got married and moved off-world. Rio knew she'd go sooner or later. He just expected it to be later."

Talan turned around on the chair. She was still naked, except for the necklace Rees had given her. The silver ball was cool against her chest.

"He was in love with her?" she asked, surprised.

"I think so."

Talan fingered the necklace. "But Shareem can't fall in love. I read that. Your emotions, like unhappiness and grief and love, were suppressed or eliminated."

Rees' expression was quiet. "That isn't true. Shareem can fall in love."

"Then why do the books say they can't?"

Rees put his fingers under her chin. "Because the books aren't written by Shareem."

Talan thought about Lady Ursula's diary, how it had cut off after the last page, and how Lady Ursula had never been seen again.

"Shareem are not allowed to leave the planet," she murmured.

"No, they're not."

"Does Rio want to leave because of Serena? Does he want to find her?"

Rees traced a soothing finger down her neck. "No. He knows he doesn't have a chance with her. He just wants…freedom."

"What about you?"

Rees leaned and kissed her cheek. His warm, silken hair brushed her jaw. "What about me?"

"Do you want to leave Bor Narga?"

He smiled. "No."

"You don't want your freedom?"

"I have freedom. Besides, there's a few reasons I want to stay here."

His smile made her shiver. Wouldn't it be nice if one of those reasons was her?

Well, she could dream, couldn't she?

"Rees."

He kissed the hollow of her throat. "I'm right here, baby."

"Is there more? I mean, you showed me so much already, and I'm not technically a virgin anymore."

"I'd say you're *definitely* not a virgin anymore."

"But is that all? Are we finished?"

He raised his head. His eyes were darkening. "Sweet baby, I can show you anything you want."

"Level one?"

"What?"

"We skipped over level one, didn't we?"

He stopped. "Maybe a little."

Talan knew she was drawing this out on purpose. She could easily tell him they were done and go home, never see him again, but she didn't want to. Not yet.

"Can you show me level one?" Her gaze drifted to the sealed door of the bathroom. "Maybe in your water shower?"

His smile returned. "You're a vixen."

"Maybe."

She smiled back at him. He leaned down, scooped her up, and carried her into the bathroom.

Hours later, she was damp and exhausted and curled up on the bed with him again. The window was going gray with morning.

"Level two, next?" she asked sleepily.

His laughter moved the bed. "You're insatiable, Talan."

That was true. She couldn't get enough of him.

Talan didn't know whether that was because he was Shareem and had gotten under her skin, or maybe just because he was Rees.

"I want level two again."

He laughed.

She sat up, looked at him indignantly. "Is something funny?"

"When you first saw me, you were afraid to touch me."

"I didn't know you, then."

Rees propped himself up on one elbow. "You asked for my DNA. That's not something a woman asks a man every day. At least not unless she's married to him and wants a kid."

"I told you, I'm doing research on Shareem."

"You really know how to flatter a guy, don't you?"

She widened her eyes. "Were you offended?"

"No. For some reason I wanted to do anything you told me."

She thought about what her computer program had showed her. "I looked at your DNA. It's human. It's exactly like mine. Well, I mean not *exactly*. You're you, and I'm me. But it's human."

"You're sweet."

"It's true. I could see where they messed with you, but it's human DNA. You're not a different species."

He went quiet. "But I'm not human, Talan."

"Yes, you are."

He gave her an impatient look. "I was created in a laboratory. I had about twenty different DNA donors, including other Shareem. That's not normal."

"Yes it is. We all are created when DNA comes together. Maybe most of us have only two donors at a time, but we have grandparents and great-grandparents and we all get DNA from them. You just got yours all at once."

"And you don't think that's weird?"

"Well, it's unusual. If you think you're special for not having parents, I was dumped in a crate on the shelter's doorstep. Can you imagine that? Being left because no one wanted to take care of you?"

He brushed a strand of damp hair from her cheek. "Lady Petronella took care of you."

"I know. I was lucky. And I love her, but it's not the same thing, is it?"

"Poor Talan."

"The point is, I don't feel special or not normal because of it. It just happened."

"That's not the same thing as people sliding your food tray in through a hole in the wall because they're afraid to come in the room with you."

She stared in surprise. "Why were they afraid of you?"

She'd never met a man as gentle as Rees. Well, okay, he hadn't been exactly *gentle*, but he hadn't hurt her, either.

Rees gave a little shrug. "People are afraid of Shareem."

The answer was evasive, but she let it go. She couldn't imagine anyone being afraid of Rees, at least once they'd gotten to know him.

Rio, yes. Rio had scared her in a way Rees did not. But Rio was level three, and maybe all level threes projected that edge of fear.

"You know what, Rees?" She pressed her finger to his sculpted chest. "I think you like being special. I think you don't want to be human."

He slanted her a look. "Oh, yeah?"

"Yeah. You want to be special, to stand out from the rest of us. To be better than us. Well, you're not. When we get home, I'll show you your DNA. You're no different from humans, Rees. I'll prove it."

He was smiling for some reason. "You are so asking for it, Talan."

"Asking for what?"

Rees growled. He hauled her up and plopped her on her hands and knees. "Say your prayers, babe. Your little ass is going to be so red."

She squealed. She tried to put her hands over her behind, but he shoved them away.

The spanking was hard. He knew how to make it sting, yet make it exciting at the same time.

"You know why women decided to get rid of Shareem?" he asked, pausing. "Because Shareem can make women stop talking. And women just *hate* that."

Talan couldn't talk at all. She could only scream and laugh and beg him to stop.

He didn't stop. He spanked her until she was out of breath, and then he rose up behind her and slid his cock into her wet and slippery opening.

After that, talking was out of the question.

It was late morning before they finally got out of bed again. Rees took her home—after he went out and bought her a new tunic to replace the one he'd ripped. It wasn't as nice as her old one, but she touched it like it was pure silk.

They'd made love all night. Rees hadn't thought Talan would be able to keep up with him, but she sure had enthusiasm.

The last one had sent her to sleep again. She'd smiled at him before she drifted off, had even murmured *thank you*.

At least she'd stopped going on about him being human. He couldn't exactly explain to her why he was different not only from humans but from other Shareem.

If word got out that R294E8S was still alive and walking around, life could get bad for Rees. It might even get short.

And Rees liked life. Especially this week.

He and Talan rode the train back to Lady Petronella's house. Talan snuggled up to him like before, and he kissed her.

A few tight-assed women gave them looks of disapproval, but Rees figured that was because Talan was getting laid, and they weren't.

Talan had certainly softened from her first, stiff-necked dealings with him. She liked him now. Last night he'd messed with her mind a little, so that she'd relax and enjoy it and he wouldn't hurt her.

But he knew that she liked him even without his Shareem spells. The thought warmed him.

He liked her, more than just a little.

Rio had gotten his heart broken by an upper-class woman. Even though he'd quickly reverted to his fun-loving ways, there was a bitter edge to him that hadn't been there before.

Rees had vowed never, ever to lose his heart to a woman, upper-class or otherwise.

And now, here he was, starting to fall for a rich girl.

Life jerked you around in weird ways.

When they reached Lady Petronella's house, Metri and the other servants were nowhere in sight. Neither was Lady Petronella.

Rees told Talan to go to her room and sleep. If she slept like a good little girl, he said, he would show her some more level two fun this afternoon.

She's smiled, kissed him, and ran off.

Talan was not afraid of him. Now that she'd lost her shyness, she smiled at him like they were friends.

But she did not realize that Rees was dangerous. Last night, he'd held back because he hadn't wanted to hurt her. He'd made her love what he did. He'd taken away the worst of the hurt.

But it had been hard to hold back. Talan turned him on in more ways than he'd ever thought possible.

The women at the lab who'd sacrificed themselves for the sake of science hadn't smiled at him warmly or given him shy looks from under their lashes. They'd let him know that it was an experiment, nothing else.

Not exactly the way to a Shareem's heart.

Rees had taught them to respect him. And fear him. He'd twisted one of them up so much, she'd helped him escape.

But even with them, Rees had never lost control. He'd always had the upper hand, always had the power, always been the master.

He needed to regain that control with Talan, or he might regret it. Even he didn't know what he could do if he totally let go.

So, he needed to teach Talan to fear him. He knew exactly how to go about it. She'd get scared and send him away, and then he wouldn't have to worry about hurting her.

Also, he had things to do, like help Rio. He needed to talk to people, get things done.

He needed to forget Talan's shining hair and sweet pussy and beautiful eyes.

Shareem could fall in love. They did fall in love.

But it was very stupid to.

Chapter Eleven

ﻼ

"You want to go to the holo-block?" Talan looked across the table at him in confusion.

He and Talan dined alone. Lady Petronella had breezed in, announced she was going out, kissed Talan, and turned to depart.

Talan had blushed rosy red, but Lady Pet hadn't seemed to notice. She'd winked at Rees, then breezed out again.

"Holo-blocks can be fun," Rees said now.

"I know, but why do you want to go back to it? You mean the one where I first saw you, right?"

"Yes. You said you wanted more fun and games, and here's your chance."

"Yes, but why go there?"

He stared at her. He was supposed to be in control here, but Talan always made him lose it. "Why not go there?"

"Because we can use the holo-room here."

He grinned. "It's not big enough. We need something big. Like a forest, or a jungle."

"There's a holo-room under the house. A big one."

"Big enough for a jungle?"

She nodded. "I used to play down there all the time. I'd go on an ocean liner. That's a huge ship that they used to use to cross the oceans on old Earth."

"I've heard of them. Big, were they?"

"The holo-room is the size of the entire first floor of the house. Is that large enough for what you want?"

Lady Petronella's house took up an entire city block. Must be nice to be rich. "Yes, I think that would be big enough," Rees said.

"Excellent. When do you want to go?"

He sensed her pheromones stirring. "Whenever you're ready, babe."

She was ready right away. He figured she would be.

Talan took him to a lower level of the house and locked the door behind them. She'd told no one to disturb her unless it was a dire emergency.

Metri, obviously used to similar directives from Lady Petronella, stoically agreed.

Talan showed Rees how to use the panel to program the block. "I haven't been down here in ages," she said. She looked about the huge, empty room and sighed. "Too busy, I guess."

Rees brushed her cheek. "You should never be too busy to play."

"Easy for you to say. But that's your whole life, isn't it? Games?"

She didn't know the half of it. "Yes. You could say that."

"So what are we going to play?"

She was ready, eager, willing.

Rees told the holo-room that he wanted a forest. Deep woods, with rustling undergrowth and cool breezes and tall trees and birds.

With a rush of sound, the forest closed in on them. Grass crushed beneath his feet as he walked, letting out a green scent.

The trees stretched away endlessly. The room was huge, and as they moved, the hologram shifted with them to make it seem like the woods ran on for miles.

All to the good.

"The game we're going to play," he said, his voice deepening to Shareem tones, "is 'you *will* run away from me'. Then I'll hunt for you."

Talan was supposed to look at him in sudden trepidation. Instead, she grinned.

"Hide and seek? I was good at that as a child. I warn you, I always won."

"We'll see about that. Now, run along."

Her grin widened. She had her hair in a braid and was wearing a sleeveless tunic, good for showing off her long legs. "Count to a hundred," she said. She loped off under the trees, then turned around and pointed at him. "And no peeking!"

Rees turned his back. He didn't need to peek.

He opened his senses, stretched them behind him. He could feel the quiet trees, and the pseudo-woodsy air, and her trail winding among the holo-scents, growing fainter as she ran.

Her trail wouldn't fade out altogether. Just enough to make him keen to follow it.

To humor her, he counted to a hundred.

He turned around. He couldn't see her through the trees, couldn't hear her either.

But he knew where she was.

His heart beat faster. His skin heated. His balls started to itch. His mind began to sharpen, blotting out peripheral thoughts, and humor, and warmth.

He sensed a woman, and he would have her.

He started walking in the direction she'd taken. He'd find her quickly. And then she'd see. She'd understand. He started to run.

A female programmer had volunteered to do this same simulation in the lab. When they'd pulled her out, she'd gasped, "He's a monster. Gods, what have we done?"

The next time they'd done a simulation—with a new volunteer—they'd locked Rees in chains first.

That had been a big mistake.

Rees' skin burned and the tunic scratched him. He pulled off his clothing as he ran, casting it aside.

Talan's trail was fairly obvious, but at a few points, he lost her. He stood with his head bent, testing the air with his heightened senses.

His skin was hot and his cock was tight and throbbing. He wanted her. He'd find her and throw her to the ground, spread her thighs, and enter her.

She was his woman, and he'd show her that.

He remembered her smirking and saying that she might ask Rio to show her a few things.

His blood burned. *No, not Rio. You are mine.*

Mine.

He found her scent again. His excitement built. His mind dimmed to everything but tracking her.

The grass tickled his bare legs as he ran through it, the scent of trees and rainwater buoyed him.

This is what he was made for, to run, to hunt. To find her.

When I find you, little girl, I'm going to make you understand what I am.

She'd come this way. He plunged through the undergrowth. She was good at covering her trail, but not good enough.

He'd be able to sense her, always and forever.

He stopped in a clearing surrounded by tall trees. He wasn't sure what kind of trees they were—some had broad leaves and others had needles. Neither grew on Bor Narga, but with a holo-room, you could have whatever you wanted.

He turned his head from side to side, feeling the air for her. His blood pumped through him, and his skin was scorching. The black chain on his left arm felt ice-cold.

She was near. Hiding.

The air was silent as though the woods held its breath.

He could scent her, waiting. He could taste his own anticipation. He'd drag her from her hiding place, make her kneel before him. His. Forever.

He'd show her what her philosophy was worth. He'd bind her to him, and she'd be happy in her bondage.

He knew he could enslave a woman just by touching her. He had done it before, but then he'd released his slaves.

He would never release Talan.

She would pay for using him, for stirring him up, for not realizing what he was.

She was near, very near…

The branches crackled above him, and suddenly something soft and womanly fell on his back. Talan wrapped her arms and legs around him and kissed him on the cheek.

Adrenaline shot through him. He grabbed her, whipped around, and thumped her on her feet.

She smiled up at him, her eyes starry, and flung her arms about his neck. "I won. You couldn't find me."

His arms closed around her back. His mind whirled in confusion. *Take her! Make her obey.*

She brushed a light kiss to his lips. "I told you I was good at this game."

Punish her. Make her beg for mercy.

No, said a voice deep, deep inside him. *Don't hurt her.*

"I love you, Rees," she whispered.

He dragged in his breath. He spoke with effort, forcing his lips to move. "Don't be stupid, Talan."

"I want to be stupid. I'm tired of being sensible."

He kissed her. His wild senses rose, blotting out his kinder self. He kissed her hard, bruising her lips.

When he at last broke the kiss, she just smiled. "I think I know what happened to Lady Ursula."

Rees didn't know, or care, who the hell Lady Ursula was. He trailed kisses to Talan's neck, bit her flesh.

"I think she stayed with her Shareem. Never went home again."

He tasted her skin. It was salty with perspiration. He threaded his fingers through her hair, breaking open the braid.

"I have a house on the second moon. My parents left it to me. It's a nice house, not so large as Lady Pet's. It's green there."

The second moon of Bor Narga. A place where the rich had resorts and beautiful views. Where a Shareem was forbidden to go.

He pulled her head back. "I hope you have a good time, there."

She looked confused. "I would take you there. We could be together there."

"I can't leave Bor Narga."

"But—"

He kissed her, his tongue in her mouth stopping her words. "Get on your knees, little girl."

She was supposed to look frightened. Supposed to beg him to let her go.

Talan smiled at him, then plopped to her knees and kissed his groin through the loincloth.

She touched it, slanted him a wicked look. "Aren't you going to take this off?"

He growled at her. He unfastened the strings, nearly ripping them off, and cast the loincloth aside.

His cock, hard and throbbing, pushed straight out.

"How big are you?" she breathed. "Have you ever measured?"

He knew how big he was. The lab researchers had written down every measurement.

"Twelve inches."

Talan looked impressed. She reached up, grasped him with both hands. A good piece of cock still stuck out past her fingers. "It's longer than both my fists put together."

She leaned forward and licked the tip.

Rees' mind went hazy. He groaned.

She closed her mouth over his cock where it protruded from her fists. Her hands remained in place, tight against his balls.

Her mouth played, her tongue dancing around his tight tip.

He stroked her hair. He tried to mesmerize her with his mind. She was supposed to be his slave, right?

All he could do was tilt his head back and enjoy the feel of her mouth on him.

"Talan, baby…"

She sucked and licked and bit—everything he'd taught her. She slid both hands around to cup his ass, and sucked him *hard*.

He drove into her mouth, groaning. Excitement whirled through him. He wanted this woman forever.

She sucked and sucked, her mouth hot and wet. He went hotter and hotter, and suddenly, his seed burst from him in one scalding shot.

Talan bucked, surprised, but she held her mouth on him, took his come.

"Sweet baby, that's right," he murmured. "Swallow me down."

She did. She swallowed it all. She licked her lips and smiled up at him.

He hauled her to her feet. He kissed her hard, tasting himself and her all mixed up.

"I want to fuck you so bad, Talan."

She kissed him back, twining languid arms around his neck. "Yes, please, Rees."

He could think of a hundred different ways to do her. He knew literally a hundred different ways, all of them good.

But he knew which way he wanted her.

He laid her down in the grass, pulled her tunic off over her head. Face to face, skin to skin, lips to lips.

Her tight cunt pulled him into her. She laced her arms around him and held him. Her eyes were heavy with wanting.

His skin was hot, his cock tight and hard. He wanted her with the animal mindlessness of R294E8S. At the same time, he was Rees wanting Talan. One Shareem wanting one beautiful, stubborn, exciting woman.

She lifted her hips, grinding against him. "Rees," she moaned.

He wanted to soothe her and kiss her, but he was too worked up. His body was taking over, his control eroding.

Her face twisted in joy. She kissed him hard, then she arched back as he pumped into her. A few seconds later, she screamed her release.

She was so damn beautiful when she did that. She said his name over and over, her voice broken. Her fingernails skimmed his back.

Oh, gods, no. Not yet.

"I'm coming, baby," he groaned, and then he spilled his seed in to her.

Talan smiled at him, her face flushed, then she pulled him down and held him close.

* * * * *

Lady Petronella requested that Talan come and see her later that afternoon. She sat Talan down on a chair that automatically shifted to conform to her torso. Lady Petronella took a seat facing her and smiled.

"Well? I assume from that satisfied look on your face that you are at last a woman who knows what it's like to be with a man."

Talan pressed her hands to her cheeks. "Does it show?"

"I know you well, dear. And I'm proud of you. You were willing to find out what it feels like to be a woman."

Talan thought of the way Rees had made love to her in the holo-room. The dark blue had spread to fill his eyes, and he'd pumped himself into her again and again.

In the end, he'd held her close against his burning skin. She'd heard his heart thumping extra fast. In a regular human, she'd have been alarmed and rushed him to the hospital.

Rees had seemed to be just fine. He'd kissed her hair and soothed her with his touch and his voice.

The grass had given her a small rash on her butt. That didn't seem fair, because it wasn't real grass, but the red and itchy patch had been real.

Rees hadn't been able to stop laughing.

He'd gone with her to her bedroom, and he'd rubbed cream on her. That had taken care of the rash.

Rees had kept on teasing her, and then Lady Pet had sent for Talan. He'd been reclining on her bed, chuckling as she left.

"So," Lady Petronella went on. "You're finished with him."

A slight pain pulled at Talan's breastbone. "Finished?"

"You've coupled with him, learned some bed games. Time to send him away and move on, I'd think."

Send him away. Yes, she knew she'd send him away after he'd taught her what she wanted to know. But it was too soon.

"I'm not ready yet."

Lady Petronella gave her a pitying look. "Talan, my dear girl, you knew when you started that this was nothing more than research. Finding out what it was you were giving up."

Talan flushed. "That sounds heartless."

"You are an affectionate girl, my dear. It is natural that you feel some fondness for Rees." She leaned forward, her stiff skirts rustling. "But he is Shareem, Talan. Shareem were not made for affection, they were made for sex. Nothing more. Pleasure without attachment. That's what made them so attractive, and why DNAmo made so much money from them."

"Shareem can love," Talan said woodenly.

Lady Pet's brows climbed. "And how do you know that?"

Talan said nothing.

"If Rees told you that, he was lying," Lady Petronella said. "I know about Shareem, I went with them when I was young. They give pleasure, and that is all. They know their business, but they are hardly like the rest of us." She sighed. "I always thought it must be nice not to be plagued with certain emotions."

"They are human," Talan flashed. "They have emotions, just like the rest of us."

Lady Pet patted her knee. "Now, dear, I know how you like to crusade. But Shareem are what they are, and they like it that way. The best thing you can do for them is to leave them alone."

Her lips felt stiff. "You mean, leave Rees alone. Let him go."

"Rees is a level two," Lady Pet said thoughtfully. "It might seem that he is affectionate at those levels. What I'd like to see you do, my dear, is go with a level three. Experience all of it. Then you'll understand what Shareem truly are."

Talan's thoughts flashed to Rio and what he'd said to her in Judith's bar. *It's surrendering and trusting, letting go. It's opening yourself. Putting yourself in the hands of another.*

She had already surrendered herself to Rees. What would it be like to surrender to Rio?

She shivered. Rio would frighten her. Rees didn't.

Lady Pet watched her closely. "Does Rees know any level threes?"

Talan nodded. "He does."

"Well then, there you are. Ask Rees to send his level three friend to you on his way out."

Again, Talan was struck with the heartlessness of it. When she'd teasingly mentioned she'd go out with Rio, Rees' eyes had darkened with jealousy.

Lady Pet was wrong. The Shareem did feel.

"You do want to experience level three, don't you?" Lady Pet went on. "I assure you, dear, it's worth it."

Talan had already learned excitement beyond belief with Rees. The idea that there was more excitement to be had seemed incredible.

"Do this for me," Lady Pet said. "Being with a level three will also cure you of this idea of affection between you and a Shareem." She shook her head. "You do take things too far, Talan."

Deep inside, a little voice told Talan that Lady Pet was right. Talan had allowed herself to care about Rees, which was a foolish thing to do.

When Rees had told her that Shareem could love, he'd been talking about Rio. And maybe Rees had not really understood what he was talking about.

If a person couldn't fall in love, could they understand what it was truly like?

Talan had blurted twice to Rees that she loved him. Both times, he'd simply shrugged it off or told her that he was making her feel like that.

And he probably had been. Shareem could relax a woman, soothe her, make her believe all kinds of things.

Perhaps she'd mistaken Shareem skill for affection.

Well, then, Rees wouldn't mind if she asked to see Rio.

Lady Petronella was wise.

She looked Lady Pet in the eye. "All right," she said. "I will send for the level three. I will experience everything. And then I will be finished."

She rose to her feet, stalked to the door, and went out, head high.

When the door closed, Lady Petronella sighed and rang for Metri.

* * * * *

Rees raised his head when he sensed Talan enter the room again.

He wanted her so much. The wanting was driving him insane. He'd never felt anything like it before.

When she'd looked at him and said *I love you, Rees,* he'd so wanted that to be her own feelings and not what he did to her mind.

He looked at her from where he lounged on the bed, gave her a smile. Her nipples were pressing against her tunic, hard as little pebbles.

When he'd first met her, she'd buried herself under robes. Now she wore the thinnest of tunics as if she weren't ashamed of her body any longer.

She knew what she was, and she accepted it.

He patted the bed. "Come and sit next to me, sweetheart."

She closed the door. She didn't come to the bed.

"You have to go, Rees," she said. "Go back home and leave me alone."

The joy drained out of the room in a hurry. "Why?" he asked. "What happened?"

"Nothing's happened." She would not look directly at him. "But we're finished, aren't we?"

"Are we?"

She was beautiful with her hair curling around her face and her folded arms pushing up her breasts.

"We are finished, Rees," she said quietly. "There's nothing more you can teach me."

Rees stood up. He'd put his own tunic back on. "Not quite, Talan."

"You are level two. I want to learn level three."

"You're not ready for level three."

"Yes, I am."

He pitched his voice to be soft and seductive. "Talan, my innocent sweetheart, you are nowhere near ready for level three."

She knew that. He could tell by the look in her eyes. But something was making her stubborn.

"I would like you to send for Rio. Tell him that I want him to teach me."

"And you are *definitely* not ready for Rio."

"You know everything about me, do you?" she asked, flushing.

He went to her. "Yeah, I do. I know you're not ready for Rio, so just forget about it."

"I don't have to do everything you say."

"Talan, don't be stupid."

"And stop telling me I'm stupid!"

He put his hands on her rigid arms, stroked with his thumbs. He felt her soften to his touch, but she remained troubled.

"What's the matter, baby? What did Lady Petronella say to you?"

She frowned. "She told me I was stupid. Not in so many words, but she meant it. And she's right. I am."

"I'm glad you admit it. Don't mess with Rio, Talan. You'll regret it."

"Fine, then, don't send Rio. Find another level three for me."

"Why are you so anxious for level three? What we've been doing isn't good enough for you?"

He saw lust well up in her eyes. No, she liked how he fucked her. She couldn't hide that.

"It was fine," she snapped. "But I want to get on with it so I can be finished and get back to my life."

"Your *perfect* life of separating your intellect from your body."

"There is nothing wrong with that! Plenty of people do it. It's purifying."

Rees tightened his grip on her arms. "You've just learned to like your body, how to not be afraid of it. Why do you want to throw that away all of a sudden?"

"It is not all of a sudden. That was my plan all along. Discover the feelings of my body, and then free myself from them."

"That's it, Talan, rub it in that you're using me."

"Isn't that what Shareem are for?"

He stopped. She glared up at him.

If any other woman had said those words, he would have said "That's right, baby" or shrugged it off. It was true, Shareem were made to be used.

They'd been made not to have strong emotions so they wouldn't care.

That's where DNAmo had fucked up. You could mess with DNA to suppress chemicals to keep away severe depression and stuff like that. You could mess with DNA to enhance other brain chemicals that made you feel peaceful.

But DNAmo couldn't suppress all emotion, no matter how much they claimed they could.

Shareem never showed emotion at DNAmo, because what was the point?

If a Shareem let himself be happy or hopeful or like someone too much, he got hurt. Better to act like he didn't care.

DNAmo thought they'd done something smart. The Shareem learned how to keep themselves detached.

So why hadn't Rees kept himself detached from Talan? From the minute he'd seen her, he'd been screwed.

The stupid one in this room is me.

And now her "I'm done with you, Rees, send in Rio" act really pissed him off.

"If you want a level three," he said, voice hard, "you don't need Rio. I'll do it."

"But you're only a level two," Talan said. She stopped. "Aren't you?"

"No."

"What are you then?" she asked faintly.

He cupped her shoulders, leaned down to put his face an inch from hers. "I'll do your level three, little girl. Better say your prayers to whatever gods you like best. They might show you some mercy, because I sure won't."

141

Chapter Twelve

ಬಿ

Talan sat alone in her study later that evening, her nerves jumping.

Rees had told her to eat dinner and then rest as much as she could, because she'd need it for the night to come.

She'd been far too jittery to lie on her bed and sleep.

When Rees had taken hold of her, his eyes had gone Shareem dark, and she knew she'd just made a big mistake.

The friendly, smiling Rees had disappeared. He'd been angry, and in his anger, he'd let her see the very dangerous man behind his smile.

Suddenly Rio seemed as playful as a kitten.

Why had Rees lied to her? Why hadn't he told her he was a level three right away?

She thought back and realized, to her chagrin, that he hadn't actually told her he was level two. She'd assumed it, and he hadn't corrected her.

She'd been with a level three all along. One who'd been holding himself back.

Oh, shit.

She'd gotten out of bed and wandered out of her bedroom. She had a suite of rooms, with a bedroom, bath, and study surrounding a small sitting room.

It was furnished in simple comfort, the decor changing as she grew from baby to child to girl to woman. She'd always loved her rooms.

Now she barely gave them a glance as she entered her study. She sat down in front of the terminal and pulled up all her research on Shareem.

She searched Rio's name and found him easily.

Level three, black hair, blue eyes, fondness for leather. "Charming," a DNAmo programmer had written. "He'll charm a lady right into his handcuffs. And then, *watch out*."

Talan could almost hear the researcher giggling as she wrote it.

She did a search on Rees.

She found nothing.

She did the search again in several different DNAmo archived databases. She looked under level threes, where she found Rio again, but no Rees.

She looked under level two, just in case. He wasn't there either, nor was he listed as a level one.

He wasn't listed at all.

She stared at the terminal, puzzled. He might have changed his name, she reasoned, when DNAmo went out of business and left Bor Narga.

She brought up a list of all the Shareem and scrolled through them one at a time. Each had a description and a holograph that turned slowly so she could see the torso of each one. They were all naked, of course.

It was a lovely catalog of beautiful men available for a lady's pleasure. She wondered idly what had become of them all.

Not one of them was Rees.

She sat back, puzzled. Rees was Shareem. He had the Shareem eyes and the Shareem physique, and the Shareem voice and touch. Rio knew he was Shareem, and so did Judith.

So why was he not listed in DNAmo's databases?

She slowly scrolled through DNAmo's data again, to see if they'd hidden him somewhere.

Perhaps, she thought, Rees wasn't from DNAmo. Perhaps some rogue company had made him.

But DNAmo's technology had been highly advanced and very secret. No one could simply make a Shareem in their basement. At least, not without everyone on Bor Narga hearing about it.

As she picked her way through the databases, she came to a folder she'd not seen before, buried among unimportant accounting files.

The folder was marked "Special Projects".

There were two special projects. One involved the creation of female Shareem, which didn't seem to have gone anywhere. They'd started too late and had been shut down before they could complete research.

The second special project was labeled R294E8S.

The file was locked and coded.

She broke the code on the first try. She stared at the screen, astonished. Then she realized that the lock had been time-stamped. It would open easily after a certain amount of time had elapsed, in this case, twenty years.

Perhaps DNAmo had decided that after that it wouldn't matter.

Talan opened the files and scrolled through them, her heart beating fast.

The R294E8S project had involved the creation of a very special Shareem. One more enhanced, more powerful, and more sexual than ordinary Shareem.

The researchers had been very excited about the project and more than one note claimed they'd make billions from it.

Shareem were all raised like normal children at first—at least, normal children isolated from other human beings.

R294E8S had been isolated even from other Shareem. He'd been an adorable child, the researchers said, and very smart.

So smart that they'd lost control of him very quickly. They'd noted several times in the files their fears that they'd done something beyond the pale, and that they should terminate it.

But the researchers hadn't had the heart to terminate a living, breathing little boy.

As he grew older, his powers increased, and when he grew into a man's body, the researchers had begun to take great interest in him.

"He is amazingly resilient," one wrote, "and changeable as a sandstorm. One minute he's smiling that incredibly charming smile, the next, he has you on your knees begging him to whip you."

Talan shivered. She scrolled through the files, one by one, mesmerized.

They'd put R294E8S into many situations to see how he'd react. Sometimes he did nothing but talk, making conversation and joking with those conducting the experiment.

Other times, he'd confound them.

Talan read one account of a female researcher who'd volunteered to go into a holo-room with him. They'd wrapped R294E8S in chains, naked, and dropped him inside.

The researcher had brought a whip with her. They'd wanted to see what R294E8S did when dominated himself.

How he'd gotten himself out of those chains that fast, no one had ever been sure. Before the eyes of the horrified watchers, he'd freed himself and turned the tables on the would-be dominatrix.

He'd made her his willing slave in no time at all. Then he'd messed up the door lock so they couldn't open the door from the outside.

For two days, R294E8S hadn't slept or eaten, and neither had the researcher. He'd held the whip and made her obey his every command. She'd done it without fighting him.

One observer had written, "I couldn't look, but I couldn't look away. I creamed more times than I can remember, watching him control her, and fuck her, and make her do to him whatever he wanted. A secret part of me wished I could trade places with my unfortunate colleague."

At last, R294E8S had opened the doors and strolled away, tossing the whip aside like he'd done nothing remarkable. He wasn't even sweating.

They'd done more experiments, with rather willing volunteers. Sometimes he would do nothing at all, just wander the holo-room in a bored manner, waiting until they let him and the disappointed volunteer out.

Then came the day he'd taken over not only the holo-room, but the entire floor of the compound with two researchers as his captives. He'd told the watchers in the cameras that if they wanted a show, he'd give them a show.

One of captives had written of it shakily in her report notes. "He played with us. He stripped us, and whipped us, and made us beg for him. The strangest thing was, I felt no shame—indeed, I was happier than I ever had been in my life. I suspect he has empathic powers to make us feel so.

"One day he made me masturbate myself with my marking stylus. I was eager to do so, happy he watched me do it.

"The day they got the doors open and freed us, I cried like a baby."

DNAmo had grown alarmed after that. They knew they could not release R294E8S into the world, like they did the other Shareem. If he did frightening things in a more-or-less controlled environment, what would he do when he was free?

They had staff meetings in which they discussed the termination of the R294E8S experiment.

Some wanted to give him drugs that would control him permanently. The problem was that someone would have to administer these drugs for the rest of his natural life.

Some suggested brain surgery, lobotomize him. A pity, because he was so intelligent, but they'd created a monster, and they had to stop him.

A few went so far as to suggest they give him a lethal injection. A quick jab with a needle, and he'd cease to be a problem. Painlessly.

Not long after one of these meetings, R294E8S disappeared.

He had seduced one of the researchers and made her his slave, and the last thing she'd done for him was help him escape.

They made a panicked search but never found him.

The news that DNAmo had created a Shareem they could not control leaked to the press and so to the public.

DNAmo was condemned by stiff-necked philosophers and the government. They lost money. Lawsuits began to be filed. DNAmo quietly folded, and left the planet and angry shareholders behind.

They'd never found R294E8S.

Talan took a deep breath. She searched the files for pictures of this mysterious R294E8S, but there were none.

She did find a description, *Six feet, eight inches tall, muscular, blond hair, blue eyes*. Not particularly helpful. Many Shareem in the records had that description.

One Shareem who did fit that description—her Shareem—was not in the records.

She looked at the name again.

R294E8S.

In her head, she took away the numbers

RES.

Rees.

A strong hand came around her and snapped off the monitor.

She turned slowly around on her stool. He was standing over her, six feet, eight inches tall, blond hair, blue eyes. He wore his tunic, strained tight over muscle. The thin black chain glistened on his bronze-colored arm.

She swallowed. "They didn't even give you a name."

He shook his head. "No."

They stared at each other for a long time. His eyes were dark blue, watching her.

"Why did you stay on Bor Narga?" she asked. "Once you were free, why didn't you go off-planet?"

"Easier to hide here. Everyone from DNAmo left, and they were the only ones who knew what I looked like."

"But you are trapped here."

He shook his head again. "At DNAmo, I never went outside. I could look through monitors but never leave the compound. Now, every day I wake up, I can go wherever I want to go, do whatever I want to do. I talk to people, I have friends. Some days, I do absolutely nothing. It's my choice."

Simple words, but she knew they were very important to him.

"Does anyone else know?"

"Rio knows."

"And he has never betrayed you?"

"He's my friend."

A simple statement, but an important one.

"But you have an ident card." She thought of the two arrogant officers who'd pressed Rio for his ident card and tried to give him a hard time.

"Yes," he said calmly. "As Rees. Rio helped me have it made. Few people ask me for it."

The officers had been keenly interested in Rio, she remembered, and had barely noticed Rees.

"Because you do things to their minds."

"I persuade them to forget about me," he acknowledged.

"You have done things to my mind."

He hesitated a long moment, then nodded. "I might have hurt you if I hadn't."

"Then I haven't really fallen in love with you?"

His pale gold lashes shielded his eyes. "No."

She touched the silver globe that hung around her neck. "When you bought me this, you were just playing with my mind?"

"I do whatever it takes."

Tears stung her eyes. "Why? Why pretend to care?"

"Because you were an innocent, and I wanted to be gentle."

"I suppose Lady Petronella asked you to."

"She talked to me, yes."

Talan stood up. Her heart beat fast with fear and anger. "You and Lady Pet decided what I needed, did you? How dare you make me love you and then take that away so casually, like I'm one of your researchers? You go on about not hurting me, but do you have any idea how much *that* hurts?"

"I have some idea, yes." He looked annoyed.

"Do *not* start preaching to me that Shareem have emotion. You obviously do not."

He came close to her. "You think so? You wanted to find out all about Shareem, Talan. I can't help it if you don't like what you found. If you'd studied Shareem as much as you say, you'd know what we can do."

"Well, no, I wouldn't, because you aren't Shareem. You are this—thing—called R294...whatever. Anything I have learned about Shareem does not apply to you, and you knew that." She tapped his chest. "You knew that all along and didn't tell me!"

"Tell you what?" he snapped. "That I'm a monster who scared the shit out of my creators?"

"You aren't a monster. I told you, your DNA is—"

"Human. Yeah, you said."

"It is. But it doesn't matter. You knew what you were, and yet you went on with it. If you really didn't want to hurt me, why didn't you just tell me to go to another Shareem, like Rio, or...or a level one?"

"I remember trying, and you not listening."

"Why didn't you just walk away? You could have at any time."

He pinched her jaw between his fingers and thumb. "Because I wanted you, Talan. I wanted you for my own."

"Don't you dare do your tricks on my brain again. I'm wise to you, R294E8S."

His eyes darkened, the irises widening. "I saw you, I wanted you, I took you. That had nothing to do with your research, or Lady Pet, or mind tricks. I wanted you because you're beautiful. So, get over it."

"You mean you did all of this so you could enjoy yourself? It had nothing to do with me?"

His grip tightened. He was so strong, she should be afraid, but she was too angry.

"No, it wasn't *all* about you, rich girl. When I saw you follow me into the holo-block that day, you turned me on in a big way. No woman ever did that before. So when I got the chance to have you, I took it. I didn't do it for your pleasure."

"You used me," she fumed.

"You used *me*."

"You are Shareem."

He stilled. "And that's what Shareem are for. Yeah, you told me."

"I was in love with you."

"No you weren't. But I—"

He stopped talking. He released her, turned and walked to the door.

Her anger blossomed into pain. "Where are you going?"

"Away. We're done."

"What about my level three?"

He stopped. His eyes had gone light blue. "I thought you wouldn't want that anymore."

She stood with her back straight. She was afraid, angry, and hurt, and she didn't want him to know it.

"Of course I still want it. If you aren't willing, I can always ask Rio."

He looked furious. "As much as you piss me off, Talan, I know you aren't ready for Rio."

"Am I ready for you?"

"No." His gaze was hard. "But you're going to get me. If you really want level three, I'll give it to you. I'll give it to you so bad you'll never forget it."

A shiver ran through her, but she stuck out her chin. "Fine."

He opened the door. "Come on."

"Right now?"

"Yes, right now. I'm ready. Are you?"

She clenched her fists, willed her knees to stop shaking. "Of course."

He held out his hand. She went to him.

He seized her hand in a rough grip and dragged her into the sitting room.

Chapter Thirteen

ॐ

Talan asked him why they weren't going back to the holo-room.

"I'm sick of holo-rooms," Rees said. "We're doing it right here, right now."

He locked the door of the sitting room. When he turned around he saw Talan standing uncertainly in the middle of the room.

He was angry at her, but her red hair, her sweet face, and her tight ass had him throbbing anyway.

She wanted level three. She was going to get it, *oh yes*, she was.

Talan's sitting room was neat and almost bare, with only a lounge and a chair with a table in between. The walls were decorated with simple paintings and souvenirs from off-world.

One of these souvenirs was a long pole made from polished wood, all decorated with carvings. He didn't know what it was for, and he didn't care.

He snatched it up. He looked at the ceiling, picked out the lenses of the three security monitors that watched the room.

He took the smooth end of the pole and jabbed it into the first lens. The plastic broke easily.

Talan gasped. Rees jabbed the second, and the third. The wires behind the lenses broke and smoldered.

"Why did you do that?" Talan asked, eyes wide.

"You don't want anyone watching, do you?"

His blood was up. He returned the pole to its place and crossed back to the door.

He'd learned about doors a long time ago. A panel to the right of it held the controls, including a mechanical switch that would open the door in case the power went out. No one needed to be trapped in a room because of a blackout.

He opened the panel, easily fused the electronic lock, and yanked out the lever for manual opening.

He was strong enough to replace the lever when he wanted to, but Talan would never be able to do it.

She couldn't leave.

She was trapped in here. With him.

Mine.

She watched him, eyes round. He could smell her fear, her anticipation.

He could also smell her lust. She was afraid, but she wanted him. She wanted him to do things to her.

Rees had prepared. After he'd sent Talan to her room to rest that afternoon, he'd returned home and gathered up his accoutrements.

He'd quietly prepared the sitting room when she was supposed to be sleeping. His plan had been to walk into her bedroom while she slept, wake her up by spanking her, and start then and there.

He'd opened the door to her bedroom, and it had been empty. Then he'd found Talan in the study, reading all about R294E8S.

Even without pictures, even without his name, he knew Talan was smart enough to figure it out.

When she'd looked up at him, she'd said, her eyes soft, *They didn't even give you a name.*

She felt sorry for him.

Even Rio didn't feel sorry for him.

Come to think of it, no one had ever felt sorry for Rees. They'd either been afraid of him or excited by him.

Talan, this sweet girl watching him and biting her lip, cared about how he felt.

This was not good.

Rees had manacles. They were thin metal and kind of pretty, but they were strong. They were made to fit snug against a woman's wrists.

He had a silver collar, too, also made to fit snug. A shiny chain hung from a ring in it.

He lifted these out of the container he'd brought with him, and slanted Talan a look.

"Come here."

He wouldn't force her. He wouldn't have to.

She took a hesitant step forward. She was shaking, the little globe hanging between her breasts trembled.

Rees slid the manacles on her wrists and locked them. She stood still while he closed the collar around her throat.

He was already hard. He pulled her to him with the collar chain and kissed her.

She kissed back, her mouth needy.

He enjoyed the kiss. He tasted her to the corners of her mouth. They wouldn't be kissing much tonight, so he savored it while he could.

She'd be too busy screaming to kiss him later.

His cock throbbed in anticipation. He took her chain and led her to a clear space on the other side of the room.

"Put your hands against the wall," he instructed. "Don't move them until I tell you."

Gingerly, Talan faced the wall and touched her palms to it.

She didn't need to be tied up. She'd stay there willingly.

Rio liked to talk to his ladies, to tease them, flirt with them, even while he was binding them. Rees liked to work silently, get down to business.

He wanted Talan to wonder what he would do, to not know until it happened.

He took a container of lube from his pack. He opened it, lifted Talan's tunic, and lubed her all over her cunt and her ass.

She looked back at him nervously. He methodically swiped the cool gel over her backside and pussy, making her even wetter than she already was. The lube blended with her cream and gave off an exciting scent.

He let the skirt of her tunic drop and put away the lube.

He wiped off his hands, then gathered up her hair. He twisted it into a soft knot and pinned it in place.

Then he took out his whip.

Rio used leather, but Rees had his specially made of synthetics. It felt soft as silk to his hands.

Talan's eyes widened. "What are you going to do?"

Rees wrapped the whip around her arms.

"Naughty girls don't ask questions," he said.

She closed her eyes. He watched the lulling effect of his voice in action. Her face and body relaxed.

"Do you want me to take off my clothes?" she asked.

"No."

He reached into his pack and pulled out a knife with a thin sliver of a blade. Talan opened her eyes just then, and gasped.

He didn't bother to reassure her. Whatever empathic abilities he had kicked in and calmed her down. Her look turned dreamy, even hopeful.

"Hold still," he said.

He sliced the tunic apart at each shoulder. He shifted the knife to her side, and drew it all the way from the inside of her arm to the hem.

The knife was so slim and his hand so precise that he slit the cloth thread by thread and never touched her skin.

He finished. She hadn't moved a muscle.

Rees pulled the tunic free. She was naked beneath it.

"You're pretty," he breathed. "*Rees is going to love you all over.*"

She swallowed and said nothing.

He put away the knife and unwound the whip from her arms. "Do you know what this is?"

"A whip," she whispered, her lips barely moving.

"It's a special whip." He took the handle in his fist and smoothed her cheek with the cord. "I had it made just for you."

"You did?"

"As soon as I met you. I went out that day and told my whip maker what I wanted. For when I met you again."

Her eyes flickered. "You planned this all along?"

"I did, sweetheart. I wanted you. I was going to find you and do you, no matter what."

"Why?"

He smiled. "Because you're gorgeous, baby. You've got the finest ass I ever did see. I wanted to whip it and fuck it and make you beg me to do it some more."

"So everything you did was to lead up to this?"

"Yes. I had fun along the way, though."

"You used me."

He turned her face to his. "Isn't that what you want? A Shareem doing what he does best to you?"

She started to turn. "You told Lady Pet—"

"Hands against the wall," he snapped. She automatically slapped them to the wall again. He brushed the whip against her cheek. "Don't let go again, or I'll have to punish you."

"I'm sorry."

"You will be." He took a step back. "Do you know why this whip is special?"

She shook her head.

"It's made of silken fibers all woven together," he said. "When I spank you with it, it won't break your skin or leave a mark."

Her mouth trembled. "Then it won't hurt?"

"I didn't say that."

He coiled the cord in his hands, stepped behind her. Her arms started shaking, but she kept her palms pressed against the wall.

"I'm going to whip you now," he said softly. "You tell me when you want me to stop, all right?"

She nodded once. She was sweating, her skin glistening under the low room lights.

He smiled to himself. His cock pushed hard at his tunic, wanting escape. *Not yet. Let's have a little fun first.*

Rees was practiced. He knew exactly how far back to stand to let the whip come down fully across her buttocks.

She flinched, drew in a breath between her teeth.

"Do you like it?" he asked. "Say yes, and I'll go easy on you."

"Yes," she babbled.

He chuckled. *Swish, snap, swish, snap.* He whipped her five more times. His blood heated, excitement pulsing.

He stopped, held the whip coiled again. "Enough?"

She let out her breath. "Yes. Yes, that's enough."

Rees stepped close to her, raked his hand through her hair, and pulled her head back. "No, Talan, it's nowhere near enough."

"But—"

"Understand me, sweetheart. I don't want you begging me to stop. I want you begging me for more. All right?"

She smelled of fear and rising excitement. "Yes."

He released her. "Now then, I asked you, is that enough?"

She hesitated, swallowed once. "No. No, it's not enough."

"You want more?"

"Yes."

"Say it then, little girl. Say *please, Rees, whip me some more.*"

She squeezed her eyes shut. "Please, Rees, whip me some more."

"You got it, babe."

The whip hissed through the air five more times. She flinched as it came down, sting on top of sting.

His cock was hurting now. He shifted the whip and pulled off his tunic then his loincloth. His cock stood straight out, throbbing and dark.

Gods, he wanted her pussy. It was wet and lubed and waiting for him.

"Spread your legs," he said.

She moved them apart, bare toes gripping the soft floor covering.

He stepped behind her, rubbed his cock against her waiting opening. He lifted her around the waist, slid her up his body, then down onto his cock.

Her pussy closed around him. She braced herself against the wall, her head thrown back. Her bound hair brushed his shoulder.

He held her tight with one arm, caressed her with his whip with the other hand. Her cunt sucked him in all the way, big as he was.

He wished he had a mirror so that he could see his engorged cock pushing up into her. He'd see his balls tight and lifted, the red curls of her pussy closing around his stem.

Rees bent his head, kissed her neck. "You're sweet, baby. You take my cock good."

She made a little noise in her throat. Her eyes were closed, her face flushed.

The chains fell against him, cool on his burning flesh.

He was way too hot. His heart was pounding. Sweat dripped down his back.

He shot his seed into her before he was even close to being ready. "That's not good," he said. "I wanted more of you."

She made a whimpering sound. "I'm sorry."

"I know you are, little girl."

He slid her off his wet cock. Her knees nearly buckled, but he hauled her to her feet with the collar chain.

He smoothed the coil of whip under her chin. "Do you want more, sweet Talan?"

She drew a breath, and nodded.

"Are you sure?" he whispered in her ear. "You must be hurting."

"Yes," she said. "I *want* it."

She did want it, he could feel it. She hadn't said that just because he told her to.

Rees steadied her on her feet. He brought up his whip and slapped her with it five more times.

He was shaking all over, his blood on fire. He could feel her pheromones and her excitement pouring over him, could even sense the hot sting when the whip came down.

"Had enough, baby?" he asked. *Please say no.*

"No, Rees. I want more."

"Then more is what you'll get." He whipped her six times in a row. She flinched at every stroke, her fingers trying to dig into the wall.

"That must be enough, now," he said.

It took her a long time to answer. He waited, his cock swelling hard, still sticky from her come.

"No, Rees, please. Do some more." She could barely get the words out.

He should stop. She wasn't used to this.

To hell with that.

He whipped her another six times. On the last one, she screamed.

The scream shot through him like a bullet. He breathed hard, sweating, his cock dying for her.

Rees had never lost control before. The researchers had always watched him, half in fear, half in excitement, wondering what he'd do if he did.

He'd paid them back by never losing control.

This was different. This was Talan, the woman he'd fallen in love with.

She'd done to him what all those scientists couldn't. He'd lost himself in her. He held the whip, but she held the real power.

He loved her.

And he wanted her, *bad*.

He snapped.

"Run from me, Talan," he said, with his last coherence.

She turned to look at him, uncertain, her body damp with perspiration. Her eyes widened when she saw his face.

"Too late," he said. He grabbed her chain. "Oh, *too* late."

"What—?"

"Get on your knees."

He shoved her down, and she dropped to her hands and knees. The silver globe he'd bought her swung between her breasts.

He got to his knees behind her. Her ass was still slick with lube and he opened her hole with his finger.

She squealed in protest.

"Take it, baby. I'm getting you ready for my cock."

She looked over her shoulder, eyes wide.

"Don't move," he said. "Don't move at all."

She looked away, went rigid.

He kept on playing with her asshole, stroking it and flooding her with soothing endorphins. He dampened her mind to turn aside everything but warm need.

Her hole relaxed and opened. He took his finger out.

She whimpered. "No, do it some more."

"No, sweetheart. What you get is *this*."

He pressed his cock onto her ass and pushed it all the way in.

The lube made everything slick and easy. But she was tight, tight, *tight*. Even through his mind-numbing, she screamed.

He rode her, pushing his cock into her tight little hole.

He'd never felt anything like it. He lost all thought but the feeling of her squeezing him. His vision went black, he couldn't see anything.

He could only smell her excited scent, could only hear her screams, could only feel her around him.

It was like being inside her skin. He braced his hands on her back, shoving his cock in as hard as he could.

She squealed and moaned. He heard other moans too, which must be his.

He wished Rio was there. He could watch her suck Rio while Rees fucked and fucked her.

Her mouth would be full of Rio's cock, and then of his come.

Her ass would be full of Rees.

He came, and filled her. His cock was too tight to want to leave. He fucked her some more, ignoring her cries.

He filled her again, and still he rocked into her, his cock hardening instantly. How much come did he have? He didn't know.

He was the ultimate Shareem. A level three, times ten.

No one had ever known the extent of what he could do. He was learning now.

He came a third time. He jerked back, letting his cock slide out of her ass.

As soon as he released her, she fell to the floor, panting.

He should stop, a voice whispered. She was an innocent, she couldn't take it.

He hauled her up by the chain, positioned her again.

"No," she moaned. "Whip me, Rees, please."

That's what he wanted to hear. Her begging him to do everything to her he wanted to.

He grabbed the chain, dragged her to her feet.

His heart beat faster than it ever had in his life. His face was scalding hot, like his cock. He felt like he was going to die.

"Rees?" Talan reached up, chain clinking, and touched his face. "Are you all right?"

Her hand was ice cold against his skin.

He'd whipped her and fucked her ass and made her his slave, and she was concerned about him.

Don't worry about me, baby, he wanted to say.

An animal-like growl came out of his throat instead.

"Rees?"

He shoved her face-first toward the wall. She put her hands on it obediently, spread her legs. He'd trained her well.

He whipped her ten times. She screamed, loud and shrill.

Rees couldn't breathe. He dropped the whip. His body temperature had soared. A normal man, even a Shareem, would be dead by now.

He staggered into the bathroom. The lights politely came on for him.

He looked around at the sterilizers and swore. No water in sight. He thought of the cool bathroom in another part of the house, the one laid out like a mountain stream. He needed that. He dropped to his knees. He'd never make it down there in time.

Talan came in, the chain making music. "Rees?"

"Get away from me," he snarled.

She took a step back, uncertain.

He still wanted her. His cock tasted her, and he felt that taste in his mouth. "Let me drink you."

"Rees—"

He got her on the floor. The tile was cool and looked like marble. It was cold against his skin but couldn't soothe him.

He spread her thighs, dipped his tongue into her wet cunt. He licked and licked, lapping her come. It was hot and salty. He loved it.

She was writhing and moaning. He licked the inside of her thigh.

He needed to stop. He'd die if he didn't stop.

He crawled away from her, rested against the cold pseudo-marble wall.

She sat up, naked and wreathed in chains, her hair coming down. Her breasts moved with her breath, and her nipples were tight and dark. Dark red curls creased the split that was her cunt.

"Get Rio," he gasped.

"What?"

"Do it. Get him on the com." Rees used the last control he had to soften her mind to him again. "If he's not at home, try Judith's bar."

"Rees—" She started to crawl toward him.

"No." He held his arms out, like he was pushing her away. The black chain on his arm was so much colder than his skin that it hissed. "Tell Rio I need him."

She watched him a moment longer, her red lips parted.

Then she nodded—*good girl*—and darted back into the sitting room. The door hissed shut, the bathroom set up to give him privacy if he needed to use the necessary. It was a well-bred room.

Rees lay against the wall, gasping for breath, lonelier than he'd ever been in his enhanced Shareem life.

Chapter Fourteen

ະວ

Rio was not at home. He was at Judith's bar. Judith said nothing about the collar around Talan's throat when she answered, but left to get Rio.

Rio's handsome, swarthy face filled the screen. His blue eyes lit when he saw her.

"Talan. You look gorgeous in chains. I knew you would."

Talan knew Rio could only see her in the monitor from the neck up, but she blushed. "Rio," she said hurriedly. "Rees says he needs you."

One dark brow went up. "Did he? Tell him I don't swing that way."

"He isn't joking." She drew a breath, trying to quell her shaking. Her butt hurt from Rees' whip, but she didn't care. "Something's wrong."

Rio seemed to catch the seriousness in her voice. "What did he do?"

"Nothing, but he's…" She hesitated, then decided to throw everything to the wind. "I found out his real name."

Rio stared at her, all humor draining from his face.

She leaned forward, whispered, "R294E8S."

"Shit." Rio reached for the com switch. "I'll be right there."

The screen went dark. Talan sat for a moment. Rio was worried. That made Talan worried.

Rees had growled at her, his voice losing its Shareem smoothness. His eyes had gone entirely blue, the whites disappearing.

His skin had flushed, becoming as stingingly hot as hers where he'd whipped it. She'd felt his heartbeat against her back, so fast she could barely separate each beat.

She'd insisted he was human, but no human could be like this and still be alive.

It would take Rio about half an hour to reach Lady Pet's, if he hurried. And then he'd have to convince Metri to let him in.

Talan called downstairs to Metri and told him to expect another Shareem.

She imagined Metri rolling his eyes after she signed off.

Rio would have to get the door open. Rees had wrenched off the manual override lever. There was another one on the other side. She should have told him that.

She had no doubt he'd get in here somehow. Shareem were amazingly resourceful.

She padded back into the sitting room, stared at the bathroom door. It was quiet in there.

Was he all right? With the marble tiles to soothe him and herself out of immediate reach, was he cooling off, calming down?

Would he return to playful, smiling Rees? Or even to the Rees who'd whispered that he'd had the whip made specially after he'd met her? Her cream had started flowing fast when he'd said that.

She'd been away from him maybe fifteen minutes, tracking down Rio and explaining to Metri.

She put her ear to the door. She couldn't hear anything within.

She drew a breath, chewed on her lip. Then she reached forward and tapped open the door.

No Rees.

She stepped inside anxiously, scanning the creamy white bathroom.

Rees crashed into her. She screamed as they landed on the tile floor, Rees on top of her.

He hadn't calmed down at all.

She understood that as he forced her legs apart and plunged his giant cock inside her one more time.

* * * * *

Rio snapped off the com, gathered his things, slung his pack over his shoulder.

"'Nite, babe," he said to Judith.

Judith turned from her customers, spoke in a low voice. "What's wrong?"

She wore a coverall open to the waist, showing the shadowy curves of her breasts. She always claimed she sold more drinks that way.

"Rees is losing his mind," Rio answered. "I'm going to help him find it again."

"Rees?"

Rio nodded. Judith frowned, like she thought he was joking. "Are you leaving right now?"

"No time like the present." Rio was worried. He'd never seen Rees out of control before, but then Rees never put himself in situations in which he'd lose control.

That was before Talan. Rio had seen the way Rees looked at her. Rees had never looked at a woman like that before, and Rio knew damn well what that meant.

Rees, that coldhearted piece of Shareem flesh, had fallen in love.

She'll break your heart, boy-o, he said silently.

"Rio." Judith wanted his attention.

"What?"

"There's a sandstorm coming. I was about to shut the doors."

Rio grinned, patted Judith on the rear. "I'll beat the sandstorm." He touched the mask on his belt. "I have my breather. I'll make it."

She walked him to the door. He chucked her under the chin. "I'll come back and tell you all about it."

Her look turned annoyed. "No, you won't. I'm still raw from the other day. When will I learn?"

"You love me, Judith."

"Go away, Rio."

Rio winked at her, walked off into the night. The air had an extra hot bite to it, and the wind had picked up. It was going to be close.

The sandstorm hit just before Rio reached the gate of Lady Petronella's mansion. All over Richville, as he termed it, servants and masters were scuttling indoors, pulling down storm doors, shuttering windows.

He saw the brown cloud hurtling at him down the wide avenue. He slipped his breath mask over his face just as the swirling winds hit.

He jangled the bell of the mansion, then pounded on the gate. The sand and wind tore at him, trying to dislodge his breather. He hung onto the gate and banged again.

Come on, no one leaves a man out in the storm.

The gates opened suddenly, and he fell inside. The gate swung shut automatically, and everything went still.

What the hell?

He slid off his mask, looked up. They had a pressure canopy overhead, a force field that kept the storm out. *Must be nice to be rich.*

Rio shook the sand out of his hair and approached the front door.

The man who answered it was short, small, and had a trimmed beard. He looked wearily at Rio. "You're the other Shareem?"

"In the flesh."

The majordomo stood aside with poor grace and let Rio into the storm-dimmed house.

The hall was empty. A staircase climbed gracefully to the upper reaches, and a decorated grille concealed the lift.

The majordomo ushered Rio into the lift and tapped the panel to take them up four levels.

The lift eased to a halt, the force field whispered open. "This way, sir," the man said as he led Rio down a wood-paneled corridor.

Real wood, Rio realized as he brushed his fingertips over is. Probably brought from some off-world nursery.

At the end of the short hall was an alcove with a door. The door was metal, painted with pleasant geometric designs in pastel shades.

"Just here, sir," the man indicated the door.

He turned to leave, disapproval evident in the set of his shoulders.

"Wait a minute," Rio said. "You were made at DNAmo, right? The perfect class of servants."

The man stopped, turned. He looked at Rio a moment, then executed a bow. "Major-Domo, level five."

Rio grinned. "Brothers under the skin. Engineered to serve."

The man looked affronted. "I *hardly* think so."

"We were both concocted out of a jar. Me for sex, you to be stuffy."

The majordomo looked down his nose. "I turned out rather well, they said. Seven clones were made of me."

"Is that so? Good on you."

The little man bowed again, stuffiness oozing from him, swiveled on his soft-booted heels, and glided down the hall, leaving Rio to it.

The locked door didn't bother Rio. He knew about doors. He figured Rees would have fused it, so he opened the panel and cranked hard on the manual lever, his muscles working.

Protesting, the door slid open halfway and stopped.

Rio walked in. He found the lever Rees had discarded, stuck it in place on that side of the door, and wrenched the door closed.

Outside the recessed window, the storm raged. The house was quiet, protected.

He sniffed. People had been having very concentrated sex in these rooms. The air was heavy with it.

Rio stashed his pack and his breather on the sofa and crossed to the bathroom. He *knew* they were in the bathroom—their pheromones screamed at him from there.

The bathroom door opened easily to his touch.

Rees had Talan on the floor. They were both naked. Rees lay on top of her, face-to-face, fucking her hard.

Rio's own cock swelled. Talan's beautiful face was twisted in pleasure. Her pale hips pressed into the floor as Rees slammed into her.

Rio went down on one knee, leather stretching over muscles, and watched them.

"Well," he said. "What can I do for you, my children?"

Talan heard Rio, but she couldn't open her eyes.

Rees was digging into her, full length, his muscular body pinning her to the cold floor.

She braced her hands on his shoulders and loved his breath on her face, the heat of his body on her.

But there was still something wrong.

Rio's voice seemed to snap something into Rees. He raised his head, saw Rio. He withdrew from Talan and lay half-on, half-off her, breathing heavily.

Rio had sand in his hair, and his blue eyes twinkled. He reached one muscular hand toward Talan.

Rees snarled. He covered Talan with his body, glared up at Rio like a lion protecting his kill.

Rio lifted his hands in a sign of surrender. "Easy there. I won't touch her. Not unless you give me permission."

"*Mine*," Rees hissed.

"Oh, so you remember how to talk." Rio's blue irises widened in the Shareem way. "Looks like those people pumped you full of adrenaline. Probably trying to trigger you with the experiments you told me about. And Talan finally did it."

Rees tilted his head, as though he were trying to understand Rio's words.

Talan said, "He's not so bad if I hold him."

She demonstrated by running her hands up and down his hot arms. He turned to her, his eyes receding the slightest bit.

"Rio," he grated. "Don't let me hurt her."

"I won't," Rio promised.

"I want her."

"I can see that. You've been fucking her all over the place."

"Control me," Rees said hoarsely. "Tell me what to do."

Rio grinned, his eyes lighting. "Now that does sound like fun. Vicarious fucking. I love it."

Rees' eyes darkened again. "Don't touch her."

"Calm down, partner. She's all yours. But you have to let me work."

Rees hesitated, his breathing still fast. His muscles tightened beneath Talan's fingers. Slowly, reluctantly, he made a brief nod.

Rio moved fast. One minute, Rees lay on Talan's body, the next, he was on his back with heavy manacles pinning his hands.

He snarled and swung his manacled fists at Rio.

Rio grabbed Talan around the waist and dragged her out of the way. He smelled of leather and sweat and sand.

"*Mine.*" Rees reached for her, but the chain between the manacles kept him from lifting his arms very far.

Rio let Talan go. She sat against the cool pseudo-marble wall and drew her knees to her chest, her chain whispering.

Rio bound up Rees' bare ankles. Rees lay on his back, growling.

Rio sat back. He shrugged off his leather top, and his muscles shadowed in the artificial light. The thin black chain around his biceps was identical to Rees'.

"Have you seen him like this before?" Talan asked him. She forgot to be shy in her worry for Rees.

Rio shook his head. "No. Usually he's Mr. Ice. Looks like you broke him."

She stared. "*I* did that?"

"You must have. Let's see if I can get him back."

Rees lay still on the marble, his cock stiff and standing straight up. He'd been trying to pull his wrists out of the manacles, and now he laid his hands on his chest, as if realizing it was futile.

He watched the ceiling, his eyes still filled with blue, his chest rising rapidly.

"Rio," she said softly. "I love him."

Rio looked at her. "You poor kid."

"Make him better."

"Are you willing to do whatever it takes?" Rio asked.

Talan nodded. She couldn't think what could be worse than having Rees die.

"All right then." Rio turned to Rees. "You hear that, my old friend? She loves you."

Rees lifted his head.

"You want her?" Rio asked.

Rees let his gaze rest on Talan. His hands and feet were bound, chains holding him, but just barely. "Yes."

"You can have her then," Rio said. "But only if you behave yourself."

Rees looked at him, gave a nod.

"Okay, Talan. Go to him."

She looked at Rio.

"He'll only do what I tell him," Rio said. "Go on."

Talan gathered the slim chain in her hands and moved across the floor to Rees. He reached for her.

"No," Rio said sharply. "Don't touch."

Rees dropped his hands back to his chest, but he scowled.

"Touch him, Talan," Rio said. "Give him a little massage."

Talan placed her palm on Rees' chest. His skin was slick with sweat, his heart hammering.

She traced his muscles, moving her finger over his sculpted pectorals and his wide shoulders.

He swallowed, his Adam's apple moving.

He was tense beneath her fingers. Rigid. *Waiting*.

She moved her hands down his arms, the black Shareem chain catching her fingers. She slid her hands around his wrists, his skin tight around the manacles.

"Touch his cock," Rio said. "Make him take it."

Talan's own body quivered in excitement. She glided her fingers around his cock, which was stiff and hot.

Rees jerked. He clenched his fists, but held them still.

Talan skimmed her fingers up and down his huge rod. It was engorged and dull red, the tip hard. She moved her touch around the flare of the head.

Rees made a noise in his throat.

"Hold still," Rio instructed. "Let her stroke you."

Rees closed his eyes. His whole body was erect, his arms and legs stiff.

Talan played with his cock, sliding her fingers up and down. She touched his tight balls, the soft skin catching on her fingers.

She thought she'd feel funny with Rio watching, but she didn't. She almost *wanted* Rio to see how she had learned how to stroke Rees, how to make him groan with pleasure.

She leaned down and put her mouth around his cock.

Rees had taught her how to suckle him, and she did it now. She laced her tongue around him, tasting him.

She sucked, teasing his balls with her fingers. Rees moved under her, thrusting a little bit into her.

She heard Rio make a soft groan behind her.

She tightened her grip on Rees. A few seconds later, he came in her mouth.

Talan was used to his seed by now. She swallowed it, wiped her mouth with her fingers.

"Gods, you're beautiful, Talan," Rio said. His irises had widened, and his face was soft.

"*Mine*," Rees growled.

Rio laughed. "I know, my friend. I'm just admiring."

Rio went to Rees then and carefully removed one of Rees' manacles. "Now, it's your turn. Touch her, with just your hand. Remember, she loves you."

Rees flexed and clenched his hand once. Then he reached out and put his fingers on Talan's arm.

His hand was hot, and it shook. But he drew it down Talan's arm, gently. He stroked up the inside of her arm, moved his fingers to her breast.

Her nipples tightened and rose. He traced the tip of her breast, flicking it with his finger.

He wasn't calm. His breath still came fast, and his body was tight. But he held himself back, touching her with utmost gentleness.

"That's it," Rio said. "Feel how pretty she is."

Rees held her breast in his hand, closing his eyes.

"Remember who she is," Rio said, his voice low and Shareem-smooth. "And how you feel about her."

Rees opened his eyes. His breath slowed the slightest bit.

"That's it," Rio said.

Rees traced his fingers over Talan's breasts and then moved up to her face. He glided his touch across her cheekbone.

"Play with her pussy if you want," Rio went on. "Show her how you feel."

Talan spread her knees where she knelt, inviting him. She kissed his fingers as he traced her lips, then let his hand move between her thighs.

He closed his eyes again as he dipped his finger into her. He softly played with her clit. She shivered, hot, and felt her cream slide over his fingers.

"You like that, Talan?" Rio asked softly.

"Yes." She closed her eyes, let her head drop back, enjoying it.

Rees fingered her, slid his hand over her cunt. Her body took over, squeezing his fingers, remembering its lessons of the past few days.

"Come for me." It was Rees talking now, his voice still broken. "Come for me, Talan."

He could turn her on just by touching her and saying her name. She spiraled into climax, arching onto his hand. "Yes, Rees, *please*."

"Nice," Rio said.

The compliment sent her higher. "Rees," she sobbed. "*Rio*."

Rio chuckled. "Hey, she remembered I was in the room."

She turned to him, still rubbing herself on Rees' hand. "Rio," she said again. "Thank you."

Rees heard her. His hand was full of her sweet cream, and he didn't care who she thanked. He wanted to thank Rio, too.

The red haze had receded from his brain. He knew he'd been fucking her, but it hadn't registered completely.

He'd come and come and so had she. He'd been lost in it, unable to think or see or hear. He'd been in a black pit of desire, unable to climb out.

All he could think of was wanting her, and fucking her until he died.

But he didn't want to take her with him.

Rio had said, *Remember how you feel about her*, and that had saved them both.

Rio knew. Rio understood Rees better than anyone. The smartass would gloat about it, but oh well.

Talan's pussy closed around Rees' fingers. Gods, he loved her pussy. It had never been touched by anyone but him.

He withdrew his hand. She whimpered, collapsed to her knees. She brought her hands up to her breasts, touched her nipples.

Rees licked his fingers, enjoying her taste. He didn't need to wait for Rio's instruction for that.

Rio chuckled again. "You're getting the hang of it, children." He moved to Rees and undid the manacle on his other wrist. "You've graduated to two hands."

Rio himself was worked up. His body temperature had climbed, and his hard cock was obvious against his leather pants.

But he simply moved aside and told Rees to go ahead. Rio was holding back, letting Rees have everything.

Rees appreciated that. He also appreciated Talan's bare and soft breasts, her pussy creaming again for him.

Rio told him to use both hands. Rees did, skimming them over Talan's body. He loved Talan's body.

He knew how he felt about her. The idea that Shareem could not love was being shot down for the ridiculous myth it was.

Rees thought about how much he loved Talan as he touched her body, teased her nipples, rubbed his fingers over her cunt, and brought her to climax again.

Rio made an appreciative audience. He said the words that Rees didn't have the voice to say, how beautiful Talan was and how lucky Rees was. Well, duh.

Rio told Talan to get on her hands and knees, instructed Rees to have fun with her ass. As long as he was nice, Rio said.

Rees asked for lube. Rio handed it to him. Rees rubbed her ass with it, opening her with his fingers. He'd done this earlier tonight, but now he was fully alert, enjoying it.

He probably could send Rio away now, but he wasn't comfortable alone with Talan, yet. He was too worried he'd go crazy again.

Rees eased two fingers into her ass, and with his other hand, pressed two fingers into her cunt.

Talan groaned with it, wriggling around his fingers.

"Do you like it, Talan?" Rio asked from his vantage point. "Almost like having two cocks in you."

Talan's answer was a moan. Rees pressed a little harder. He was on his knees now. He leaned down and kissed her smooth back.

"Rees," she whispered.

"I'm here, baby," he said.

He pushed a third finger into each of her holes. She let out a little cry, then settled down to enjoy it.

"That's it, Talan," Rio breathed from across the room. "Feel it."

She was. She pulsed around Rees' fingers, squeezing them hard. She threw her head back, and came, her body writhing.

Rees slowly withdrew his fingers. His cock throbbed. "Let me," he whispered.

He was not asking Talan, he was asking Rio.

"Slowly," Rio said. "Remember how you feel about her."

Rees nodded. He knew damn well how he felt about her.

Talan wanted him. Still sobbing with her release, she lifted herself on hands and knees. "Please, Rees," she begged.

Rees set his hands on her soft, lovely hips, and pushed the tip of his cock inside her cunt. He stayed there for a minute, feeling her sweet pussy surround him and pull him in.

He let himself inside, inch by slow inch. Talan writhed and groaned and begged for him.

Rio moved so that he could watch Rees' cock slide into her and see her face while she took him. But Rio didn't touch. He sat with his arms folded, his eyes alone taking all the pleasure.

Rees buried himself to the end of his cock, closing his eyes and feeling her. Talan was beautiful and tight and wet and *his*.

How did he feel about her? Tender, and excited, and for the first time in his life, happy.

He knew it couldn't last, but he could enjoy it now. The mindlessness of it receded, and he consciously enjoyed himself in Talan.

"She's beautiful, Rees," Rio said.

"I know." Rees moved himself inside her. "I know."

Chapter Fifteen

ဢ

Talan thought she'd die of joy. He'd opened her so wide with his fingers, and now his cock had taken their place.

She came, pulsing around him, feeling him press still harder into him. His hands on her back were hot, but no longer burning.

Rio watched her, his eyes intense. She remembered how she'd fantasized about him watching her and Rees in the bathroom at Judith's bar.

Fantasy or premonition?

Whatever it had been, they were all three enjoying it—Rees slowly pumping her, Talan squeezing him, Rio watching it all. The air held a tang of sex and sweat and leather.

She wished the night could go on forever.

Rees spilled his seed into her, groaning with the pleasure of it. He laid Talan down on the floor and backed off.

She sank down, exhausted, but did not close her eyes. She did not want to fall asleep. Not with Rees there to pleasure her and Rio to watch. She wanted to be awake for every minute of it.

She loved Rees. It was not just Shareem tricks with her mind, she *loved* him. She would explain it to him when they were finished, when they were calm.

Rees sat next to her, raking his hands through his damp hair. "Damn, Rio, I want to fuck her again."

"Of course you do." Rio came to him and removed the chains from Rees' ankles. "Let her ride you."

Rees smiled. She loved his smile.

He wrapped his arms around her, lifted her tired body. He lay down on his back and positioned her to straddle him.

She was exhausted, but happy to be surrounded by his arms. He guided her hips down, just sitting her on the tip of his cock.

"You take it from here," he said.

His fever had gone. He was smiling at her, a softness in his Shareem-blue eyes, looking just like he had when she'd first met him.

Talan was tender now, but she still wanted to feel him. She slowly lowered herself on his cock, letting her knees and thighs take her weight.

The tendrils of her loosened hair brushed her shoulders, sensuous as his touch. She lowered herself further, further, wanting all of him.

She settled fully on his cock. He lifted his hips, sending it deep inside her.

Instinctively, she rocked, feeling his cock all the way in. She licked her lips, dug her fingers into his chest.

She loved him inside her, wanted nothing more than this. He excited her and intrigued her and made her feel so happy. She understood now what Lady Pet had tried to explain and what Lady Ursula had meant in her diary.

There was no feeling in the world like being in the arms of someone you loved. That feeling wasn't wrong, or shameful, or restricting.

It was freeing, and joyous, and wonderful.

She rocked on him, and he held her steady with his hands. He smiled at her, his eyes calm and loving.

"Talan." He said her name in his Shareem voice.

She leaned down and kissed him.

He pulled her to him by her collar chain. He held her there, kissing her, moving inside her.

He smiled at her, and she laid her head on his strong shoulder.

His hands roved her back. He soothed her with his Shareem touch, his skill reasserting itself over her mind.

She smiled happily as his fingers moved to her ass. He spread her a little.

"Rio," he said.

She looked at Rees in surprise.

Rio quickly pulled off his leather pants and his loincloth and stood up, naked. "Thought you'd never ask."

Before she could grasp what would happen, Rio was behind her. She felt his fingers on her ass, cool with lube.

She stared at Rees. Rees smiled. "It's all right, baby." He touched her hair, and she suddenly knew it *was* all right.

Rio tossed the lube aside. His touch was as soothing, his voice as mesmerizing. "Don't worry, Talan," he said. "I'm just taking my reward."

Talan thought she'd be afraid, thought it would hurt. Rees held her steady, spreading her.

When Rio pressed the tip of his cock against her hole, she tensed.

The two of them touched her and murmured to her, calming her down.

She relaxed, laying her head on Rees' chest, loosening herself, trusting them.

Rees was still inside her, still hard. Rio's cock started its slow journey in. He was hard and engorged, excited from watching and anticipating.

Rio moved in slowly, soothing her with his hands. Talan kept still, feeling every inch of him as he slid, slick with lube, into her tunnel.

Rees stroked her hair, murmured her name. Rio took his time, his thighs closing around her, the heat of his body covering her back.

And then he was in. Gods, he was all the way in. Both of them were, spreading her, filling her. She screamed.

"Shhh, baby," Rees whispered.

"She's beautiful, Rees," Rio rumbled behind her. "Tight and beautiful."

Talan screamed again, for pure pleasure. She felt both cocks in her, one in her anus, the other in her pussy. They were both hard, both pulsing, both so near each other, yet not touching.

"Tight," Rio repeated. "So damn tight."

She felt Rio's lips on her back, his hands stroking her.

Rees kissed her. She lost herself in his mouth, in his kiss, in his touch. His cock moved in her.

Rees possessed her. Rio played with her. Their cocks moved in and out, the pleasure so intense she couldn't stand it. She couldn't *take* it.

She must have screamed that, because Rio kissed her skin and Rees smoothed her hair again.

"Yes, you can," Rees murmured. "You can take it, Talan. You're my good girl."

"She's a sweetheart," Rio said. "Best ass that's ever swallowed me."

Talan could only make incoherent noises. Rio laughed. "She likes us."

She *loved* them. Rees kissed her. His balls rubbed against her pussy as he rocked his hips. Rio thrust in slow rhythm, his slick cock sliding in and out.

Rees held her face and looked into her eyes. "You're beautiful, love."

They'd clouded her mind, making her warm and relaxed and at the same time, tight with excitement.

She loved them both. She was grateful to Rio for helping Rees, for pulling him back from insanity.

And she loved Rees. She loved him, and she would never ever stop. He might think he'd twisted her emotions to think so, but she knew the truth.

She loved him.

She always would love him.

She came, twisting and writhing, her mind dark with pleasure. They held her, keeping her soothed, keeping her from hurting herself.

"I love you, baby," Rees whispered.

She pulled those words in, savored every one.

"Fuck," Rio said. "I'm coming. I wanted to stay here all night."

His words died into a groan of satisfaction. He pumped his hot seed into her, then stilled, his hands on her back warm and shaking.

"Rio," she whispered.

He leaned forward as he withdrew, kissed the nape of her neck. "Thank you, sweetheart."

Then he was gone. Talan cried out at the loss of the warmth on her back, the fullness in her ass.

But Rees took over. He drove himself hard into her, while Rio sat back and watched.

Rees' hips moved. "Love you," he said, while she screamed her pleasure.

He shot his seed high into her, saying her name over and over, telling her he loved her. Rio was next to her again, smoothing her hair, touching her skin, kissing her neck while Rees rode out his climax.

Then it was over. Rees gathered her in his arms, and she settled down on him, with him still inside her. He was sweating and hot, his arms shaking as he held her.

Rio stroked her back, then lay his head on it, brushing little kisses to her skin.

Comforted by her two Shareem and exhausted from passion and worry, Talan fell asleep.

When she came awake, they were all in the sterilizer, Rees holding Talan on her feet while he carried on a conversation with Rio.

She couldn't hear what they said through her sleep-fogged mind, but Rio laughed every once in a while.

They'd removed her chains and the collar. She was as bare as a newborn baby.

Rees must have noticed she was awake. He leaned down, planted a kiss on her cheek and smiled at her. "Hello, sleepyhead."

He sounded his normal self. Well, as normal as a man called R294E8S who had been made to be the Shareem that surpassed all other Shareem could sound.

"Ready for bed?" he asked.

She nodded. She could sleep for weeks.

Rio rumbled with laughter. "Poor baby. Having to be slammed by Rees all night."

Talan smiled. She wrapped her arms around Rees' strong neck. "Was nice."

Rees lifted her into his arms. "She likes me," he informed Rio.

Rio laughed again.

This was what Talan liked. Laughter and love and the warmth of Rees.

Rees carried her out of the sterilizer and through the sitting room to her bedroom. He laid her on her bed, which came alert and moved to conform to her body.

Rees hugged her in a way no bed could compete with.

Rio had followed them. He was still naked, his cock still hard, the black hair at the base of it a smudge in the dim room.

185

He leaned over and gave Talan a kiss on the lips. "Sleep tight, pretty girl."

Rees' kiss lasted longer. "Thank you, baby," he said.

She touched his face. He was handsome and gentle and rough, and she loved him.

Rees stood up. Talan snuggled down in her bed, liking the fact that two very handsome, very naked Shareem stood over her bedside.

She saw Rees and Rio exchange a glance. They looked down at Talan again.

Then, to her everlasting happiness, they climbed into the bed with her and took her together once more.

* * * * *

When Rees emerged from the bedroom an hour later, Rio was already dressed and packing up his gear. Behind him in the bedroom, Talan had sunk into profound slumber. Rees left her to sleep. She needed it.

Rees pulled on his tunic, sat down on the Spartan sofa in the middle of the room. He was exhausted. Even R294E8S had his limits.

"Rio," he said. "I owe you one."

Rio's face split into a grin. "I think I got some recompense."

Rees lowered his voice. "I told you I'd help you get off-planet. And I will. I have some contacts I'll see in the next couple days."

Rio sat on a chair. Leather stretched across his arms as he rested his elbows on his knees. "I don't know, Rees. Maybe I shouldn't go."

"You should. You hate it here."

Rio sighed. He glanced at the closed door to the bedroom. "I'll tell you what, if I had a girl like her, I wouldn't go anywhere."

Rees' reaction was instinctive and swift. "Leave Talan alone."

Rio chuckled. "You've got it bad, buddy boy. Don't worry. She's yours."

Rees calmed himself deliberately. "Is she?"

"I saw how she looked at you and heard what she said. She had fun with me, but it's not me she wants."

"She doesn't want me either," Rees said. "At least, she doesn't need me, whatever she thinks she wants."

"You so want to make this complicated, don't you?"

"I'm Shareem, Rio. She's upper-class. The two don't mix. Look what happened tonight. I can't be sure that won't happen again."

"You were pretty wild," Rio admitted. "But hey, I can always come over and calm you down."

"Not if you go off-world, you can't. And I won't make you stay here so you can control me with Talan."

"If it had been any other woman, I'd have just thrown you in a holo-pond somewhere. But she's worth it. I hope you realize that."

Rees looked at him. "I'm not that stupid, Rio. I know what I feel about her. So, what do you think is the fastest way to ruin a sweet girl's life? Pair her with R294E8S."

"That's not who you are anymore. You're Rees."

"A name I gave myself."

"You gave yourself everything," Rio said. "A name, freedom, a life. Who else was going to give it to you? That's the man she cares about. Not some Shareem experiment."

Rees sighed. He leaned against the sofa, which was doing its best to make him comfortable. "She doesn't know what she cares about. She has a head full of ideas and thinks she knows all about life. Now she'll think she knows all about sex."

"Not if you stick around and keep teaching her."

Rees said nothing.

Rio knew he was fighting a losing battle. He shook his head. "You're stupid sometimes, Rees."

Rees gave him a look. "You want it to work out with me and Talan because it didn't with you and Serena."

Rio shrugged. "So? I figure one of us should be happy."

"You will be. You'll get off-planet to some green world and get yourself four or five women of your own. They won't know what hit them."

"Hey, if you're giving up Talan, maybe I'll stay. If you don't want her, I can always visit."

Insane jealousy rose up inside Rees. He suppressed it with effort. "She doesn't need you, either."

"Hey, she seemed pretty happy with me not half an hour ago."

No.

"We're both leaving her alone," Rees said. "You're going off-world if I have to pull in every contact and favor to make it happen."

Rio held up his hands. "It's your loss, boy-o. A beautiful woman *and* your best friend."

"My *only* friend." Rees stopped. It was true. Rio was the only person, besides Talan now, who knew who Rees really was. Rio had never betrayed him, never made life hard for him, never acted like he feared him. They were friends. Period.

"I'll miss you, Rio," Rees admitted. "But your ass is out of here."

"Aw, and I didn't think you cared."

"Shut up."

Rees got to his feet. He collected his things, including the collar that had adorned Talan's neck. He was tempted to linger and touch it, remembering how beautiful she looked in it.

He stuffed everything in his pack. "Come on," he said to Rio. "It's done."

Chapter Sixteen

ဆ

Lady Petronella was reading her letters when Talan made it to the morning room for a very late breakfast.

Talan sat gingerly, wincing as her tender bottom touched the seat.

Lady Pet looked up, sent her a knowing smile. "You must have had a good night."

Talan blushed. The footman placed a plate in front of her, and she dug into the food. She was very hungry.

"*Two* Shareem," Lady Pet went on once the footman had departed. "Absolute bliss. We'll have to get the security cams repaired, but I imagine it was worth it."

Talan thought about Rees and Rio in her bed at the last, how they'd held her between them, kissing her and touching her, their bodies warm and comforting.

She thought about Rees telling her that he loved her.

"Yes," she said quietly. "It was worth it."

"Well, I am pleased to hear that. No more turning up your nose at beautiful men, eh?"

Talan ate without answering. The mysterious Lady Ursula had been right all along.

She finished off her fruit, sipped the chilled, flavored liquid in her glass. "Did Rees have breakfast earlier?"

"I don't believe so, no."

"He was not in his room." Talan set down her glass. "I thought perhaps he'd walked Rio to the station."

Lady Petronella gave her an odd look. "No, Talan. Rees is gone."

For a moment, Talan didn't register what she said. Then all the feeling drained out of her limbs. "What do you mean, gone?"

Lady Pet carefully set down her letters. "I saw him earlier this morning. By himself. He told me you were finished with him, and he was going home." She looked at Talan. "Oh, dear. You didn't know this."

Talan couldn't answer. She remembered how Rees had kissed her for the last time, his hand gentle in her hair. "Good night, little girl," he'd whispered.

"He asked to speak to me this morning." Lady Pet's eyes held pity. "He told me you had finished, that he'd taught you all he could teach you. I had assumed you were in agreement."

Finished. As if what they had could be finished with a shrug and a smile.

Rees was right, Talan supposed. She'd asked him to teach her. And he'd taught her. Now it was time for both of them to move on.

The coldness of that struck her. Talan squeezed her eyes shut and balled her hands on her lap.

She heard the swish of Lady Petronella's robes, and then Lady Pet pressed a light kiss to Talan's hair. "Oh, my dear. I am so sorry."

"You warned me," Talan said stiffly. "You said I was too affectionate."

"I know, dear. But I had no idea you were going to lose your heart."

"I was stupid."

"No, darling. It's never, ever stupid to fall in love."

Lady Pet was wrong. It was the most foolish thing Talan had done in her life. She'd been curious, she'd wanted to touch fire.

Well, she had touched it, and now it burned.

She raised her head. The silver globe that Rees had bought her brushed her skin. She unclasped the chain, drew the trinket off, and opened it.

The holo-lights played, red and violet and brilliant gold and soft yellow. The patterns danced and twisted 'round on themselves. It was a cheap trinket, but a thing of beauty.

Talan closed the globe, shutting out the lights, laid it on the table, and quietly left the room.

* * * * *

As the days passed, a part of Talan thought that Rees would come back, if only to say goodbye in person.

Talan rehearsed meeting him again. She would quietly thank him for his time and shake his hand. She'd promise him that if he ever needed anything, she would be happy to help him.

She'd be dignified, sophisticated, and above all, not a crying, clinging, silly woman.

She would keep everything cool and impersonal.

Days turned to weeks. Rees did not come back. He did not send her a message. He'd cut the tie, neatly and thoroughly.

Talan knew where he lived. She could journey to the city, look for him in his apartment. She could place a com call to him. She could call Judith at the bar and casually inquire if her friends Rees or Rio were there.

She could do all those things, but she didn't.

The wild time she'd spent with Rees became another of her memories, and her life went on.

She'd meant to write up her experience with her Shareem in a diary, similar to what Lady Ursula had done, but whenever she tried, she found the memories too painful to touch.

Her body healed, but her heart remained raw.

She received an invitation to go on retreat with her sisters in the Way of the Star. They would travel to a remote town in the desert, where they'd meditate and study and listen to lectures.

Talan jumped at the chance. She packed her sun-robes and fled.

She spent two months in the sanctuary trying to find peace. She meditated, she chanted, she studied, she learned.

But whenever she looked at the stars looming over the empty desert, she'd wonder if Rees had managed to get Rio off Bor Narga, and toward which star Rio had gone.

When she meditated through a gazer, which zoomed in on a specific star, she'd wonder if she'd ever calm her raging emotions to be as still as her body.

When she listened to lectures about separating mind from body, she remembered Rees explaining that Shareem learn to live in their bodies fully, integrating body and mind into a perfect whole.

She tried desperately to forget all about Rees, and as the two months drew to a close, she pretended she had.

She returned to her home with Lady Petronella and decided to have a grand clear out. She went through all her books and vids and either threw them away or gave them to charity.

While Talan sorted through her study one afternoon, she came upon Lady Ursula's diary.

She nearly threw it in the recycler. But on impulse, she sat down, put the disk in the reader, and cued up the first entry.

She read the diary all the way through. Lady Ursula made her laugh when she described her first meeting with her Shareem, how nervous and excited she was.

Lady Ursula went on to recount how she felt when Brandt first spoke her name, how it felt to touch him.

The Shareem have strange eyes, she wrote, *so intense and changeable. One moment they're light and playful, the next, dark with wanting.*

Rees' eyes had been like that.

An entry much later in the book read—*I have fallen in love with this man. He touches me like no other person in my life. I cannot decide if the emotion is mine or part of the soothing chemicals he emits.*

The last entry said—*We have come to the end. There is no more time to decide. My life will never be the same again.*

Lady Ursula had written no more. Talan could find no records of her after the last date in the diary.

Lady Pet had not known what had become of her. She was no longer in the social directories or even the directory for the city. She had simply ceased to exist.

Talan flipped back to the beginning of the files. Twenty years ago, Lady Ursula had been fairly young, about twenty-five. She would hardly be an old woman now.

Talan sat up, her heart beating faster. She checked the city database of anyone who had popped up new twenty years ago, around the time of the end of the diary. Lady Ursula could simply have changed her name.

She found no one who might have been Lady Ursula. She also found no evidence that Lady Ursula had moved off-planet. People left an amazing number of records behind them wherever they went, but Lady Ursula had not.

So, she stopped looking for Lady Ursula.

She looked for Lady Ursula's Shareem instead.

She easily found Brandt's record in the databases of DNAmo and also registered with the city.

The city had record of where he lived, but she did not have the clearance to make the database spit up his address.

But she knew someone who might point her in the right direction.

She ordered the litter and her bodyguards, filled up her breather, told Metri she was going out, and let the litter take her down to the old city.

* * * * *

When Talan walked into Judith's bar, everyone in the interior stared.

The day she'd come here with Rees, in her short-sleeved tunic, her hair up, holding Rees' hand, no one had paid her any attention. She'd been just another girl with a Shareem.

Now she was obviously upper-class, fully swathed in robes, descending from a hover litter. She left the bodyguards outside.

The first person she saw was Rio.

Talan stopped, surprised. She'd come to see Judith, thinking that Rio would be gone by now.

Rio stood up, held out his arms. "Hey, rich girl." He gathered her to him in a hard hug.

Talan thought about her last meeting with him, and her face heated, but she was in too much of a rush to worry about it.

"Rio," she said. "Can I talk to you?"

He grinned. "Any time, babe." He locked his arm around her and led her to a table in the corner. Judith, with a smile of welcome, brought them drinks.

Rio grinned at Talan and leaned toward her. "Please tell me you want me to fuck your ass again."

"No. Although—" she moved her glass, blushed "—that *was* nice."

"It was *more* than nice. But what did you want to ask me?"

"Whether you knew a Shareem called Brandt. A level one."

Rio lifted his brows. "I know him. Not well."

"Do you know where he lives? I want to talk with him."

He looked still more perplexed. "Why do you want a level one after you've had a three?"

"Because I want to ask him a question," Talan said. "If you know where I can find him, please tell me."

Rio drank his ale, closed his hand over hers. "I'll do better than that. I'll take you there."

He led her to an apartment that was not far from the bar. They walked, Talan telling the bodyguards to take the litter and go to a nearby rest station to wait for her.

The day was hot, with the sun scorching overhead and the wind dry and scalding. Talan's sun-protective clothes helped, but she was still sweating by the time they reached a somewhat faceless white building.

A little courtyard in the center, unprotected by shields, provided tiny relief from the heat. The courtyard held a fountain and greenery that someone obviously cared for.

Brandt lived in the apartment at the back of a breezeway. Rio rang the buzzer and the door opened right away.

"Rio?" A tall man with Shareem-blue eyes gazed at them from the doorway. He had chestnut brown hair and his face bore the sculpted handsomeness of the Shareem. He was obviously older than Rio, but not by much.

"What brings you here?" he asked Rio. He was curious, not unfriendly.

"My lady does," Rio said. He put his arm around Talan. "She wants to ask you something."

Brandt gestured them inside. "Come in out of the heat. What can I do for you, my lady?"

Rio ushered Talan through the doorway, then the door thankfully closed against the heat.

Talan brushed the sand from her robes. "Actually, I wanted to ask—"

She stopped. A lady had come through a door behind Brandt. She was a pretty woman in her forties, dressed in a sleeveless tunic. Her brown hair, which bore only a thread or two of gray, had been pinned up in a casual twist.

She looked at Talan, and her brows rose the slightest bit.

"Lady Ursula?" Talan asked.

The lady smiled. "I used to be called that. Who are you?"

"My name is Lady Talan d'Urvey. I am Lady Petronella d'Naris' adopted daughter."

Her look turned astonished. "You are Lady Pet's daughter? My, how time flies. I saw you once at a charity ball. You were a tiny girl, so adorable." She smiled, returned to the present. "What brings you here?"

"This." Talan pulled a disk from her robes. "It's your diary. I found it when I was researching."

Lady Ursula took it gingerly. "My diary." She looked at it a moment. "Oh, my. I forgot all about this."

"What is it?" Brandt asked in his Shareem-deep voice.

"I wrote everything down about how I met you." Lady Ursula's cheeks grew pink. "And the few weeks after I met you."

Brandt looked intrigued. Rio grinned. "Ooo, I'd like to read *that*."

"No," Talan, Brandt, and Lady Ursula said at the same time.

"Fine." Rio held up his hands. "Everyone gets to have fun but me."

Talan ignored him. "The diary ended, but—" She looked from Lady Ursula to Brandt. "It didn't end, did it?"

Brandt slid his arm around Lady Ursula's waist. She snuggled back against him. "No. It didn't," she said.

"You stayed with him," Talan said.

"She did," Brandt answered. He pressed a kiss to Lady Ursula's hair. "Lucky for me."

"I loved him," Lady Ursula said simply. "When I realized that, I packed my things, said goodbye to Lady Ursula and social acceptance and came here to beg him to let me stay."

Brandt smiled. "Which I did. Gladly."

"You've never regretted it, have you?" Talan asked.

"No." She touched Brandt's cheek. "Never."

"I'm glad," Talan said softly.

"Did Lady Petronella send you down here?" Lady Ursula asked. "To look at Shareem? She was the only one I knew of who didn't pretend that Shareem did not exist. She was always an odd sort, was Lady Pet."

Talan gave her a pained smile. "She still is an odd sort. But no, I really came to give you your diary. And discover whether you had a happy ending. I'd hoped so."

"I did." She patted Brandt's hand where it rested on her waist. "I highly recommend falling for a Shareem." She glanced at Rio. "Is he the one for you?"

"No," Talan said quickly.

"I hope not," Brandt said.

"Hey," Rio protested. "Standing right here!"

"No," Talan said again. "It's Rees."

Brandt's eyes widened. "Rees?"

Lady Ursula looked puzzled. "Have I met him?"

"No," Brandt answered. "You'd remember if you had. He's mysterious as they come, even for a Shareem. Are you sure, Lady Talan?"

"She's sure," Rio said. "She could have me, but no. She's gone on Rees. Go figure."

Lady Ursula smiled again. "Well, I hope you'll be very happy together."

"Thank you, Lady Ursula. Please be well."

Lady Ursula gave her a little bow. "You follow the Way of the Star, I see. Be well, sister."

Brandt said goodbye in the normal way. He and Rio exchanged good-natured insults, and Rio led Talan away.

She caught a glimpse of Brandt pulling Lady Ursula into his arms before the door shut.

Chapter Seventeen

ℬ

"Rio, please help me find Rees."

They walked out of the courtyard, back to the main street. "I don't know where he is, Talan," Rio said. "When Rees doesn't want to be found…"

"I thought he was helping you." She glanced around, lowered her voice to a hiss. "Helping you go off-planet."

"He is. But contacts are one thing, money is something else. The better my chance, the more it's going to cost. I haven't come up with enough yet."

Talan looked at him, startled. "I didn't think of that. If you need money, Rio, you can have all you want."

"What—?"

"As my gift to you," she said. "I want you to be happy. But right now, we must find Rees."

"I agree. But like I said, he's hard to find when he doesn't want to be. I haven't seen him in a couple of weeks."

She dropped the hem of her robe to the dust. "Do you think he's gone?"

"Gone where? Shareem can't leave the planet." Rio shook his head. "He does this, sometimes, Talan. I don't know where he goes. He just goes."

"But he comes back."

"Eventually."

She picked up her skirts, gave him her best Lady Talan look. "Then take me to his apartment. He'll have to come back there sooner or later. I'll wait."

Rio looked her up and down. "You're as crazy as he is," he announced. "But all right."

She waited in his apartment for two days. Rio offered to stay and keep her company, but Talan said no.

Rio tempted her, but she wanted to be alone when Rees returned. She didn't mind snuggling into Rees' bed, burying her face in the pillow he used, showering in the water shower that cleansed his body.

She told Lady Pet what she was doing, and Lady Pet, while not cheering her on, did not stop her, either.

"Follow your heart, darling. But come home soon. I love you, too."

Talan kissed her fingers and pressed them to the screen, then turned off the monitor.

By late afternoon of the second day, she was restless but determined to see Rees again, to talk to him, to explain.

It would not be dignified to grab him by the tunic and babble to him what she'd decided, but to hell with dignity. Dignity meant loneliness.

She was lounging on the sofa, reading books from his small collection, when she heard—or thought she heard—his step in the hall.

She put down the book, crossed to the door, and opened it.

She saw no one. In the corner, the lift tube was rising.

"Rees?"

Her heart beat faster. He couldn't have known she was waiting in his apartment, could he?

Would she be fool enough to chase him down the street? She thought maybe she would.

She hastened up the emergency stairs and into the foyer. It was likewise empty. She rushed out into the narrow street, looked up and down.

The street was unusually deserted, but she swore she heard footsteps hurrying around the corner. She ran to look.

The sandstorm, predicted all morning, swept at her from the other end of the street. Before she could even run back around the corner again, it was upon her.

Her breather, the apparatus meant to save her life, was hanging by the door in Rees' apartment.

Sand choked her. It tore at her robes, trying to peel them off her. She could not see, she could not hear.

She groped for the nearest wall, thinking she could follow it to a doorway. But as much as she crawled, she could not find a wall. She fell to her knees, reaching desperately for sanctuary.

I love you, Rees.

She thought it as hard as she could. She'd never have the chance to tell him, but maybe her thoughts would linger here.

Rees had showed an ability to read emotions. Maybe he'd be able to read hers on this corner in the dust.

She crawled, her lungs burning for air. The skin on her hands and face grated away, blood stinging.

She kept crawling, her sense of survival hoping that maybe, just maybe, she'd bump into a doorway before her lungs gave out.

Someone grabbed her, hauled her up from the ground. A hand pulled her head back by the hair, and a breath mask was shoved onto her face.

She gulped air. Breath-mask air always smelled musty, but at the moment it was the like sweetest perfume she'd ever known.

The strong hand held her steady, and then suddenly removed the mask.

At first she panicked, and then the mask came back. She took another breath of air. The mask went away again. She understood. Her rescuer was sharing his mask with her.

She held onto him. His body was hard and tall, and she knew he was Rees.

Her heart beat hard with joy. His arm went around her, and he pressed the breath mask over her face.

He pulled her with him into the sand. She went willingly, knowing that even with the breath mask, they had to get indoors.

A door was only a few yards away. The breath mask was over her nose and mouth when the door opened and the two of them stumbled inside.

They were in the foyer of his apartment building. She must have crawled down the length of the street, not toward a building at all.

Her heart froze as she contemplated how near death she'd come.

She lowered the breath mask, brushed the sand from her eyes. Her hand came away with a smear of blood.

"Talan." Rees scooped her to him, holding her hard.

"I was waiting for you," she said, her voice grating. "I thought I heard you."

"You did hear me. Gods, Talan, I never thought you'd follow me with a storm coming."

"I forgot about the storm. I've been reading books. Why didn't you come in?"

He smoothed her hair from her forehead. "Let's go downstairs."

He would not say anything further. He got them both downstairs then led Talan into his bathroom and turned on his water shower.

With hands as gentle as only Rees could make them, he undressed her and got her into the shower.

He stripped down himself and entered the shower with her. He used a cloth to clean the blood from her face and hands.

Talan started to shiver. She was cold, and the water falling over her body held a pleasant warmth.

Rees was gorgeous when wet. His hair was dark with water, and water beaded on his lashes. His skin was slick and cool. His cock had already risen, and water clung to the dark blond curls surrounding it.

"How did you know I was here?" she asked.

"I can sense you," Rees said, his Shareem voice, even neutral, working its magic. "I've always been able to sense you."

"So you went away. You didn't want to see me."

He looked at her. "No, I didn't."

Her heart felt like there was a hole in it.

He wiped the blood from her face, put the cloth aside. He stood there looking at her, his wet body inches from her own.

She couldn't help herself. She drew her fingers down his hard-muscled arm, bumping them over the little chain that said he was Shareem.

She had no courage, but she made herself speak anyway. "I came to tell you that I love you, Rees."

Rees shook his head. His eyes had darkened, but he held himself from her. "You feel what I made you feel. I can make you think you are in love."

"I haven't seen you for nearly three months," she said. "Can your Shareem suggestions last that long?"

He shrugged, muscles working. "We had a lot of sex, Talan, in your rooms. Rio was there, too. It probably lingered."

"That's what you think, Mr. Shareem. I've been away for two months, in the middle of the desert sea, in a cloister with a dozen women. You cannot tell me that your Shareem empathy or chemicals or whatever it is can span two thousand miles and eight weeks."

That stopped him. He frowned.

"You see?" she said. "You don't know everything. When I was out there, alone, meditating, I realized I love you. I love you deeply. And not just because you put a spell on me."

"Talan—"

She folded her arms. "Stop talking, please. You woke me up, Rees. You made me realize what it was to live and to feel, and not just think. You made me realize I wanted love in my life, and that I wanted it with you."

He put his hands on her shoulders, using his Shareem touch to loosen her. "Talan, I'm—"

"Shareem. I know. And more than Shareem. You're the infamous R294E8S. But you know what?" She stood on her tiptoes, cupped his face in her hands. "You're all of those things, but you're not any of them either. You're *Rees*. And I love Rees."

"Baby—"

"I'm not finished. Lady Ursula gave up everything to be with her Shareem. And she never regretted it one jot. She defied convention, and she's happy. Lady Pet defies convention. I used to be embarrassed by her, but I've realized convention can stifle and cheat you of life. I don't want that."

She kissed his parted lips. "I want you, Rees. I want your smile and your beautiful body and the way you want me to feel good. I would give up everything I have for that, even live in a hovel. What am I giving up, anyway? The chance to live a cold life with cold people who turn on you the moment you put a foot out of line? I don't want that. When I was out in the cloister, I realized that. I want warmth, and I want you, and I want to love you, and I want—"

Rees put his hand over her mouth. "Talan, would you stop talking for three seconds?" He let out his breath. "I love you, too, baby. But I don't want you living in a hovel. Can you understand that?"

She nodded. She reached up and pried his hand away. "We don't have to live in a hovel. I have lots of money. We can live wherever we want. We can live here. It's nice."

He started to laugh. "This from a woman whose furniture rearranges itself for her."

She waved that away. "Oh, it doesn't matter. I want to be with you, Rees, not my furniture."

He held her face in his hands. His touch was warm, soothing, entrancing. "But remember what happened? I nearly went crazy with you. There's nothing to say that won't happen again."

"What calmed you down? Rio?"

"Partly." He smoothed his thumbs across her skin. "Mostly remembering that I loved you."

"Well, then. All you have to do is remember that you love me."

He smiled, the shower water dripping down his face. "That easy, is it?"

She gave him a sly look. "Well, we could always ask Rio to help out."

His eyes darkened. "You're mine, Talan."

She kissed him, and the kiss turned deep. He gathered her to him, his hands sliding down her slick, wet back.

She felt his heartbeat quicken, his tongue roughen inside her mouth.

She broke the kiss. "Are you sure about that?" she teased.

He growled low in his throat. "*Mine*, baby. All mine."

She slid her arms around his neck. "Besides, Rio's going off-world."

"Only if I can get him there."

"I told him I'd provide the money for it. All you need do is set it up."

Rees looked down at her, brows raised. "You'd do that?"

"Why not? He helped you when you needed it. He probably saved your life. I'm happy to help him out."

Rees held her close. "You're an amazing woman, Talan."

She lifted her face to his. "Does that mean you want to stay with me?"

"Hell, yes." He kissed her, his hands moving to her ass. "Every day of my life. Gods, Talan, I don't know what you did to me."

"Whatever it was, I like it."

"You can't change your mind now." His voice became lower, sexy, enticing. "I let you go once, and it nearly ripped me apart. I can't let you go a second time. I hope you came to stay."

"Of course I did. With you."

"Because I'm not letting you go. I'll keep you chained up if I have to."

She smiled, excitement fluttering in her belly. "That sounds like fun. Level two, is it?"

He growled. "Whatever I am, that's what you're getting."

"Good." She nuzzled his cheek. "I can't wait."

He lifted her against the cool wall of the water shower, and moved her legs apart. "This is what you're getting, babe."

He slid his cock inside her. She was wet, not only from the water, but from her own cream that had started flowing as soon as he'd pulled off her clothes.

This was where she belonged, with his arms around her and him inside her.

She wriggled, letting his cock penetrate deep. "Do you still have the collar?" she asked.

His eyes had filled with dark blue, his breath was hot. She swore that steam was curling from his skin. "You bet I do, little girl."

"I want to wear it. I want to hand you the chain and be your slave."

His cock pressed in deeper. "I think I can arrange that."

"I want you to fuck me every day, and teach me to fuck you."

"You got it, baby."

"Do you love me, Rees?"

"Gods, *yes.*"

He ground his hips into her. She tilted her head back, let the shower rain on her. He kissed her throat, licked her skin.

"Will you whip me when I'm bad?" she whispered.

He bit her neck. "Every time."

"I want to be bad, now."

Rees licked his way back to her lips. His fingers slid between her buttocks, started playing with her ass. "I'm glad Rio's leaving. I want you all to myself."

She gave him a playful look. "But maybe we can have him over, just to say goodbye."

Rees rested his face against hers. "You *are* a bad girl."

"I know. You taught me how to be."

He kissed her hard. "I love you, Talan."

"I love you, Rees."

Rees looked at her a long moment. Then he eased himself out of her and turned off the water shower.

He took her hand, led her, dripping and naked, to the bedroom. He took the collar from where he'd kept it beside his bed and snapped it around her neck.

She pulled the thin chain across her breasts, letting it catch on her hardened nipples, then she handed it to him.

His eyes went dark. He took the chain and led her with it across the room to the terminal.

Then he sat her on his lap and turned on the monitor to call Rio.

* * * * *

Hours later, she drowsed in Rees' bed, sandwiched between her lover and her friend. Both men warmed her, soothed her, eased her.

Her legs were twined with Rees' and her head lay on his shoulder.

This is happiness, she thought. *Love and being* with *the ones you love.* Not ideas, not riches, not convention. Deep contentedness, she thought, was worth all that.

She nearly laughed out loud thinking about *how* she was spending time with the ones she loved.

Her soft giggles woke Rees and Rio. Rio raised up on his elbow and grinned.

Rees kissed her. He lifted her, his hands going to her already wet pussy to spread her and ready her.

And then they made her happy all over again.

Why an electronic book?

We live in the Information Age—an exciting time in the history of human civilization, in which technology rules supreme and continues to progress in leaps and bounds every minute of every day. For a multitude of reasons, more and more avid literary fans are opting to purchase e-books instead of paper books. The question from those not yet initiated into the world of electronic reading is simply: *Why?*

1. *Price.* An electronic title at Ellora's Cave Publishing and Cerridwen Press runs anywhere from 40% to 75% less than the cover price of the exact same title in paperback format. Why? Basic mathematics and cost. It is less expensive to publish an e-book (no paper and printing, no warehousing and shipping) than it is to publish a paperback, so the savings are passed along to the consumer.

2. *Space.* Running out of room in your house for your books? That is one worry you will never have with electronic books. For a low one-time cost, you can purchase a handheld device specifically designed for e-reading. Many e-readers have large, convenient screens for viewing. Better yet, hundreds of titles can be stored within your new library—on a single microchip. There are a variety of e-readers from different manufacturers. You can also read e-books on your PC or laptop computer. (Please note that

Ellora's Cave does not endorse any specific brands. You can check our websites at www.ellorascave.com or www.cerridwenpress.com for information we make available to new consumers.)

3. *Mobility.* Because your new e-library consists of only a microchip within a small, easily transportable e-reader, your entire cache of books can be taken with you wherever you go.

4. *Personal Viewing Preferences.* Are the words you are currently reading too small? Too large? Too… ANNOYING? Paperback books cannot be modified according to personal preferences, but e-books can.

5. *Instant Gratification.* Is it the middle of the night and all the bookstores near you are closed? Are you tired of waiting days, sometimes weeks, for bookstores to ship the novels you bought? Ellora's Cave Publishing sells instantaneous downloads twenty-four hours a day, seven days a week, every day of the year. Our webstore is never closed. Our e-book delivery system is 100% automated, meaning your order is filled as soon as you pay for it.

Those are a few of the top reasons why electronic books are replacing paperbacks for many avid readers.

As always, Ellora's Cave and Cerridwen Press welcome your questions and comments. We invite you to email us at Comments@ellorascave.com or write to us directly at Ellora's Cave Publishing Inc., 1056 Home Avenue, Akron, OH 44310-3502.

erridwen, the Celtic Goddess of wisdom, was the muse who brought inspiration to storytellers and those in the creative arts. Cerridwen Press encompasses the best and most innovative stories in all genres of today's fiction. Visit our site and discover the newest titles by talented authors who still get inspired - much like the ancient storytellers did, once upon a time.